Enter
Ross MacKenzie's
next brilliant world...

SHADOWSMITH
Ross MacKenzie

THE NOWHERE EMPORIUM

Kelpies is an imprint of Floris Books
First published in 2015 by Floris Books
Seventh printing 2016

The publisher acknowledges subsidy from
Creative Scotland towards the publication
of this volume

 This book is also
available as an eBook

British Library CIP data available
ISBN 978-178250-125-1
Printed & Bound by MBM Print SCS Ltd, Glasgow

*For Aileen, Selina and Mollie, my Sunshine
Girls, who light up each day.*

And for Lucy Nicholson.

PROLOGUE

THE SHOP FROM NOWHERE

The shop from nowhere arrived with the dawn on a crisp November morning.

Word travelled quickly around the village, and by midday the place was abuzz with rumour and hearsay.

"There were four shops in the row yesterday. Today there are five!"

"Did you hear? It sits between the butcher's and the ironmonger's…"

"The brickwork is black as midnight, and it sparkles strangely in the light!"

By evening time, a curious crowd had begun to gather around the mysterious building. They jostled for position and traded strange and wonderful theories about where the shop had come from and what it might sell, all the while hoping to catch a glimpse of movement through the darkened windows.

The shop was indeed built from bricks the colour of midnight, bricks that shimmered and sparkled under the glow of the gas streetlamps. Blocking the doorway was a golden gate so fine and intricate that some wondrous spider might have spun it. Over the windows, curling letters spelled out a name:

There was a glimmer of movement in the entranceway, and a ripple of excitement passed through the crowd. And then silence fell – a silence so deep and heavy that it seemed to hang in the atmosphere like mist.

The shop's door swung open. The fine golden gate turned to dust, scattering in the wind.

The air was suddenly alive with a hundred scents: the perfume of toasted coconut and baking bread; of salty sea air and freshly fallen rain; of bonfires and melting ice.

A dove emerged from the darkness of the shop and soared through the air, wings flashing white in the blackness. The enchanted crowd watched as it climbed until it was lost to the night. And then, as one, they gasped. The black sky exploded with light and colour, and a message in dazzling firework sparks and shimmers spelled out:

THE NOWHERE EMPORIUM
IS OPEN FOR BUSINESS.
BRING YOUR IMAGINATION...

The writing hung in the air just long enough for everyone to read it, and then the words began falling to the ground, a rain of golden light. The crowd laughed in delight, reaching out to catch the sparks as they fell.

Everybody who'd gathered outside the Emporium was entranced. No one had ever seen a spectacle such as this. One by one they walked forward, touched the sparkling black brickwork, examined the tips of their fingers. And then they stepped through the door to find out what was waiting.

Two days later, when the shop had vanished, a stranger arrived in the village. He was polite, and he paid for his room with stiff new banknotes. But something about him – his startling height perhaps, or the hungry look in his cold blue eyes – troubled the villagers.

He asked questions about a shop built from midnight bricks.

But the tall man couldn't find a single person in the village who could recall the Emporium.

Within a day he too was gone, and all trace of these strange events faded from the history of the place.

Those who'd walked through the Emporium's doors had no memory of anything they might have seen inside. More importantly, none of them recalled the price of admission – the little piece of themselves they'd given for a glimpse at the Emporium's hidden secrets and wonders.

Bring your imagination, the sign in the sky had requested.

CHAPTER 1

A CHANCE ENCOUNTER

Glasgow, present day

"Look out! Coming through!"

"Oi!"

"Watch where you're goin', wee man!"

"Sorry!"

Daniel Holmes darted through the Saturday shopping crowds in Glasgow, pushing and twisting and weaving. His lungs burned and his legs ached, but he did not stop. He couldn't stop; Spud Harper and his gang were chasing him. And everyone in the children's home knew that if Spud Harper was after you, you didn't slow down.

Daniel wheeled left at a butcher shop, almost

slipping on a blood-red puddle. He turned into a narrow street lined with old buildings housing fashion boutiques, restaurants and coffee shops. Carved stone angels and gargoyles seemed to watch the street from high above.

Daniel's head swung right to left. Where next? He wondered how far he was from the bus station. He imagined jumping on a bus headed to the coast, where he could stow away on a boat and escape from Glasgow and St Catherine's. Somewhere with no Spud Harper would be nice.

"Not crying for your dad?" Spud yelled at him from somewhere back among the crowds. "You were wailing like a baby in your sleep again last night. The whole home heard you! 'Daddy! Daddy! Don't die, Daddy!' Ha, ha! Don't worry, wee man, when we're through with you, you'll have something else to cry about!"

Spud and his gang were bigger than Daniel, and faster and stronger. Sooner or later they'd catch him. He sprinted across the street, jinked into the nearest shop and slammed the heavy door shut. He clutched at his chest and watched through the darkened glass of the door, crouching out of sight. He could hear Spud's gang shouting as they thundered past.

"Where'd he go? Where is the wee weasel?"

"Must be up here!"

Daniel's shoulders sagged. He closed his eyes and breathed deeply. The air was infused with the jumbled perfume of furniture polish and dust, and something like melting chocolate. Then he opened his eyes, and for the first time became fully aware of his surroundings.

The shop was a cave of wonders. Everywhere he looked, Daniel saw something he wanted to pick up, to hold, to have as his own. Silver and gold and crystal gleamed and sparkled in the light of a spitting fire. Intricate wooden clocks and mirrors of varying size and splendour covered the walls. Tiny fish flashed like bars of copper in a glass tank. There were porcelain dolls and wooden soldiers; rusted swords; stuffed animals; columns of books as high as the ceiling; jewels that seemed to glow with a silvery light. A stuffed polar bear sat in one corner, eyeing the shop like a watchman. Even particles of dust, caught in a bar of sunlight, seemed to glow like stars.

"How did you get in here? We're closed!"

The voice startled Daniel. In the far corner of the room stood a grand desk with feet carved like an eagle's talons. Behind the desk sat a small man in a dusty suit. His wavy brown hair was wild and tangled, falling over his handsome face. On the desk in front of the man lay a battered book. His hand hovered over an open page, clutching a fountain pen. He stared at Daniel with eyes the colour of thunderclouds.

"Sorry," said Daniel. "Didn't mean to bother you. Someone's chasing me." As he spoke, his eyes were drawn to the book on the desk, which had begun to tremble against the dark grain of the wood, as if there was something in the pages trying to get out.

The man in the suit frowned. He glanced from Daniel to the book and back. Then he snapped the book shut, locked it away in his desk, and got up and marched past Daniel to the door.

"See?" he said, pointing to a sign hanging on the door that read CLOSED. "Closed." He tried the door handle, opened the door. "I could have sworn I locked it." He spun back to face Daniel, staring at him through narrowed eyes. "Who's after you?"

"Big boys. From my children's home."

The man raised an eyebrow.

"You are an orphan?"

Daniel nodded.

The fire snapped and cracked.

"What happened to your parents?" said the man.

Daniel thought this was an odd question for a stranger to ask, but he didn't want to be thrown back out into the street, so he answered.

"Dad was a fisherman. Died at sea. Mum only lasted a couple of years after that."

This seemed to satisfy the shopkeeper.

"And why are these big boys after you?" he said. "There must be a reason."

Daniel folded his arms. "Yeah, there is a reason. They're goons. Spud and his pals think they run the home. They take things from the other kids – important things, like reminders of their parents and stuff. And nobody ever stands up to them. But I couldn't take it any more. I followed them. I found out where they kept their stash. I got everyone's stuff back and I explained that if the other kids stick together, Spud and his gang can't get to them. Spud didn't like that."

The little man in the dusty suit jutted out his bottom lip and nodded, disguising a smile. "Ah. Bullies. I see." He wandered around from behind his desk. "What is your name?"

"Daniel. Daniel Holmes."

"Well, Daniel Holmes, I know how it feels to live life in the shadow of a bully. We have that in common."

"Really?"

"Mmm hmm. I'll tell you what. You can wait in here until you are sure Spud and his gang are gone."

"Yes, sir. Thank you."

"It's no trouble," said the man in the suit. "Now, if you'll excuse me, I have business to attend to."

He turned and wandered towards a velvet curtain of rich, deep crimson at the back of the shop. As he reached for the curtain, he paused.

"Daniel, do you have a favourite animal?"

"Animal?" Daniel thought for a moment. "It's a bit weird," he said, "but I like magpies. People say they're the cleverest of the birds. There's a rhyme about them…"

"Ah," said the man in the suit, "one for sorrow, two for joy?"

"Aye, that's the one."

"Very good," said the shopkeeper. He smiled to himself, then said, "Well, I must be off."

"See you," said Daniel. "Hey, maybe I'll come back and buy something from you one day."

A fleeting smile crossed the man's face. "Oh, I wouldn't be too sure. Return customers are very rare in this place."

And with that he was through the curtain and away.

Daniel peered out of the window, which was tinted sepia so that the outside world looked like an old photograph. Grey Glasgow rain had begun to fall in fat drops. Puddles were already gathering on the road.

Spud Harper and his gang were long gone, but Daniel was keen to have one last look around before he left. He wandered towards a table scattered with metal toy soldiers. He picked two of the soldiers up, imagining that one was himself and the other Spud Harper, and staged a fight between the two.

Daniel's soldier was about to throw Spud off the table when something startled him, a soft, fluttering sound. He dropped the toys and stared at the red curtain to the back of the shop. Another flutter. The curtain waved gently.

He edged forward, his heart racing. When he was close enough, he reached out a trembling hand and slowly ... gently ... touched the material.

A burst of red velvet, the sound of flapping wings, and two silver birds exploded from behind the curtain. Daniel ducked and spun, and the birds flew across the store and landed on a column of stacked books.

They were magpies. But they were like no magpies Daniel had ever seen.

They were made of brilliant, gleaming silver.

Every feather, delicate as a shaving of ice, reflected the flames of the coal fire. The silver magpies fixed him with shining ruby eyes, twitched their heads to one side.

"How?" whispered Daniel, treading softly towards them, though they did not shy away as he advanced. When he was close enough, he reached out a hand. "Are you real?"

His fingers touched upon the cool silver of one of the magpie's wings. The bird let out an indignant call and flapped away, leading its twin back towards the curtain. But when they reached the rich red velvet, the birds did not fly through. Instead, they exploded with a flash, and a shower of rubies rained down on the shop floor.

Daniel's mouth hung open.

"What's going on out there?" came the shop owner's voice from behind the curtain. "What was that sound? Nothing had better be damaged!"

Suddenly unsure of exactly what he'd seen, or what kind of a place he'd stumbled upon, Daniel made for the door. A little bell sang as he dashed out into the rain and down the street.

A moment later, the short man in the dusty old suit stepped from behind the curtain. He stared around the shop. Then he leaned over and plucked two of the magpie rubies from the floor, rolling them between his thumbs and fingers. His hands closed around the stones, and when they opened once more, the magpies were sitting in his palms, brilliant silver, almost glowing in the gloom.

The man in the suit released the birds and watched as they circled the shop before settling once again on a column of books. Then he smiled a wide, clever smile, and disappeared back through the curtain.

CHAPTER 2

THE RETURN CUSTOMER

Daniel returned to the shop the very next day. He couldn't help himself.

On reflection, he felt silly for rushing out in such a panic. Now he'd had time to think, he supposed what he'd seen must have been a clever trick, an illusion, and nothing more. But he found himself desperate to know exactly how the owner of the shop had made the magpies seem so real.

He spent breakfast trying not to look at Spud Harper, who made threatening gestures at him across the dining hall for the entire meal. Slipping out during the rush after breakfast was easy; lost in the flow of the crowd, Daniel darted along to the kitchens, where the back door was always open to let out the reek of chef's cooking.

The world was bathed in Sunday sunshine, the sky endless blue. Daniel retraced his steps from the previous trip, passing the butcher shop, breathing the smell of sawdust and raw flesh, and found himself back in the gargoyle-lined street. For a moment he was worried that he'd dreamt the whole thing, but then he saw black bricks glistening in the light of the sun, and a grand arched doorway and golden sign.

The CLOSED sign was still displayed in the door. Daniel stared at it, arguing with himself, knowing that he shouldn't try to enter. But something about the shop was pulling him in. His hands trembled as he reached for the handle. The door was not locked; he pulled it open and felt warmth spilling from the shop. Inside, it was exactly as he'd left it. There was no sign of the owner, no hint of the silver birds. Daniel examined the column of books where the magpies had landed. Then, treading softly, he made his way towards the red velvet curtain, to the spot on the floor where the birds had fallen and smashed into rubies. The light in the place was dim. He had to drop to his knees to inspect the floor.

Not a single ruby *anywhere…*

The velvet curtains flapped, and Daniel found himself staring at a pair of grey leather shoes. He looked up, into eyes the colour of angry thunderclouds, eyes that did not leave him, not even for the briefest moment.

Silence.

The shop owner's brow furrowed. He rubbed at his temples. He opened and closed his mouth several times, but no words escaped. He blinked, turned around, and retreated through the curtain. Then he poked his head back into the shop, as if checking to see if Daniel was really there. Eventually, he burst through the curtain and stood inches from Daniel, stooped over so that they were eye to eye. He smelled like the pages of old books.

"How can I help you?" he said. His voice was calm, but the look in his eyes suggested that a storm was erupting somewhere in his brain.

"Erm…" Daniel said, "I just wanted another look around. Is that OK?"

The man craned his neck so that his face was even closer to Daniel's. He narrowed his eyes and whispered, "You remember this place?"

"*Yeah.* I was only here yesterday—"

The man grabbed him by the wrist and rushed him over to his desk. "Have a seat," he said, pushing Daniel into a wooden chair, sitting himself on his desk. He pressed the palms of his hands together. "What do you remember?" he said. "Tell me exactly."

"I ... I remember everything: the books and the mirrors and the clocks ... meeting you ... the silver magpies—"

The man held up a finger to quiet Daniel. His eyes were darting about the place.

"How is this possible?" he said.

"I'm sorry," said Daniel in confusion. "Have I missed something? How is what possible?"

The man leapt to his feet.

"Which children's home are you from?" he asked.

"St Catherine's," said Daniel. "It's only a few streets away."

The man nodded. "Have you ever noticed strange things happening around you? Lights flickering, mirrors smashing, that sort of thing?"

"No! Why?"

"No reason," said the man with a casual wave of his hand. Then he grabbed Daniel and pulled him from the chair, ushering him towards the door. "Listen, Daniel Holmes ... we're closed, as the sign on the door so clearly states. So I think you should be toddling off home."

"But..."

And with that Daniel was pushed out into the street, completely stunned by what had just happened. On the other side of the glass, the owner stared at him for a moment, and when Daniel blinked he was gone.

Daniel began to trudge back down the street, hands in pockets, aiming kicks at the occasional stone. If he had looked around at the correct moment, he might have noticed the door of the Nowhere Emporium opening a fraction, and an ashen hand tossing two silver birds into the air. He might also have noticed that these birds flew from rooftop to rooftop, perching on stone angels, watching his every step as he made his way back to St Catherine's.

CHAPTER 3

AMBUSHED

The thing about Spud Harper was that he *never* let anything go. Any time he had a grudge, no matter how small, he'd carry it around for as long as it took to get even. As. Long. As. It. Took. Daniel knew this. Everyone did. He might have escaped Spud once, ducking into the Nowhere Emporium, but he'd been looking over his shoulder ever since.

Daniel didn't leave St Catherine's at all over the next few days. Every time he was alone in a corridor, or turning a corner in the playground, he expected Spud to jump out at him. It didn't happen. Not that way.

Monday went by. Nothing.

Then Tuesday.

Wednesday was the same.

And the longer it dragged on the more it seemed certain that Spud's revenge would be truly horrible when it arrived.

Thursday.

The last Thursday of every month at St Catherine's was fire drill day. It happened right after lunch; you could set your watch by it. When Daniel's class sat down at their desks after the break, their teacher Mr Pimm did not even bother telling them to open their textbooks. Sure enough, a few minutes later, the air was split by the shrill of the alarm, and the class filed out, merging in the main corridor with several other classes.

Daniel's stomach sank to somewhere around his knees as he felt someone huge appear at his side. Smitty, the biggest boy in Spud's gang, smiled down at him.

"Don't say a word, wee man, or I'll knock you out."

He grabbed Daniel by the arms while the teachers were focused on getting the kids outside, and bundled him across the corridor to the gym hall.

Spud was waiting in the centre of the hall. Smitty dragged Daniel towards him and held him in front of Spud, who stuck his freckled face right in Daniel's.

"Thought I forgot about you, pal?" he said. "Thought I was gonnae let you off with what you did?"

Daniel said nothing. He stared at Spud, hatred burning in his veins.

"Here's what's gonnae happen," said Spud. "You're gonnae steal back all the stuff it took me so long to get from the other kids. And if you don't, I'm gonnae smack you once for every single thing you cost me. That's a *lot* of punches, Daniel."

Daniel stared around the gym hall. The door back to the corridor was blocked by another of Spud's gang playing lookout. No escape that way. But the back door, the one behind the stage...

Daniel brought his foot down as hard as he could on top of Smitty's. He heard the big guy howl in pain, felt the grip of his huge arms soften. Daniel managed to squirm away, taking off towards the back of the hall.

"Hey! Get back here!"

Daniel ran up the stairs to the stage. He ducked through the curtain, the sound of Spud's trainers on the boards just behind him, down another set of steps and out to a narrow corridor.

"Not this time, Danny boy!" yelled Spud. "You're gettin' it!"

Daniel ploughed on, his feet barely touching the floor as he ran to the end of the corridor and burst through a fire exit to the car park at the back of St Catherine's. Then he was away through the gate to the streets beyond, pushing past office workers who were out making the most of the Glasgow sunshine during their lunch breaks.

Daniel glanced over his shoulder, kicked into

another gear, and tore through a pedestrian courtyard between two office buildings, firing out the other side like a bullet.

"Daniel!" Spud shouted. "Stop. You're gonnae get—"

The tail of Spud's sentence was cut off by the blast of a car horn, and Daniel realised, in one of those strange instances when time seems to slow down, that he'd run out onto a road.

He heard the screech of tyres, saw the car coming towards him head on, caught the driver's horrified gaze behind the windscreen. He knew it was too late to stop, knew he was not fast enough to keep going. There was no doubt in his mind that he was going to die in the street.

A flash of silver in the corner of his eye.

Someone pressed the play button on the world. Everything screamed back to life. Before the car could hit him, something else did, knocking him sideways. He landed heavily and stared up through blurred eyes at the cloudless sky.

He was aware of someone standing over him, a person in a grey suit. Whoever it was, they were talking to him, but the voice was very far away.

The only thing Daniel wanted to do was go to sleep.

The world around him was lost to blackness.

CHAPTER 4

THE MONSTER

Edinburgh, December 1878

The knock on the door of Castlefoot Home for Lost Boys came at precisely five minutes to midnight.

At first, the call went unanswered. The man at the door waited patiently, flicking gathering crystals of falling snow from his shoulders. After a while, he took up his silver-topped cane and rapped hard on the door three times.

A minute or so passed before flustered footsteps could be heard from within, and the sound of jangling keys and heavy locks.

The door swung open.

The man inside was wearing a nightgown. He was

stout and fat-necked, a neatly trimmed beard the only evidence of where the chin ended and the neck began.

"Can I help you?" he asked, frowning over a pair of spectacles.

The visitor nodded. "I believe so. Are you the master of the orphanage?"

"I am," said the master. "And who may you be?"

The man at the door, who had been standing a step below the master, stepped up, so that they were standing on level ground. He was much taller than the average man – over six feet in height, with powerful shoulders and a square-set jaw. His neatly cropped silver hair and goatee seemed to sparkle in the warm glow of the lamps. His eyes were cold, icy blue.

"I am here about the boy," he said, his voice barely more than a whisper.

After a moment of hesitation, the master's eyes widened.

"Yes," he said. "Yes, please come in. Get out of the snow. Warm yourself."

The tall man nodded once, stepped into the Home for Lost Boys. It might have been warmer out in the snow.

"Can I offer you a drink, mister..."

"Sharpe. Vindictus Sharpe. No drink, thank you. Best see the boy as soon as possible."

"If you don't mind my saying, Mr Sharpe," said the master, "you may have picked a more reasonable hour to visit."

"The asylum does not wish to draw attention to the boy," the tall man replied. "Such cases attract stigma. Unless, of course, you wish the child's ... condition to become common knowledge?"

The master shook his head. "No, no, this will do fine!"

"Very well," said Vindictus Sharpe. "This boy ... he has been here since birth?"

The master nodded. "More or less."

"And have these ... incidents ... happened regularly?"

Again the master gave a nod. His face had transformed at the mere mention of the boy, taken on a haunted, hollow sort of look.

"Do you think you can do something about it?" he asked, clasping his hands.

Sharpe raised an eyebrow. "May I speak with him?" he said.

The master picked up a lamp and led Vindictus Sharpe through the entrance hall to a caretaker's office, where he picked a large key from a hook on the wall. After this they walked a passageway adorned with the grand portraits of previous masters and beneficiaries of the home.

"Watch your step," said the master as they began to descend a dark, twisting staircase. The stairs opened out to another corridor, this one lit by a solitary gas lamp. The place smelled of damp and dirt, and faintly of disinfectant.

"You keep him down here?" said Sharpe.

The master, who was a pace or two ahead, turned, and his face was a white mask of shame. "We've no choice," he said. Then, almost as a way of apology, he added, "He is very well fed. And we let him out into the open air once a week. There are many children in this city who have it much worse."

Sharpe did not answer.

They reached a door at the end of the corridor. The master took the rusted key and placed it in the keyhole. It was stiff, and it took him a few attempts to open the lock. He reached for the doorknob, but Sharpe's gloved hand blocked him.

"I think I will take it from here," he said.

The master stared for a moment. "Alone? Are you sure?"

"You are welcome to wait here," said Sharpe. "But, if I am to evaluate the boy, then yes, I must speak with him privately."

In spite of the cold, the master wiped a bead of sweat from the end of his nose.

"Very well," he said. "If it is necessary, I suppose. But I will be here by the door should you need me."

Vindictus Sharpe's mouth twitched. It may have been a smile, but he had turned towards the door before the master could properly tell. He reached for the handle and slowly opened the door.

The room beyond was small and square. The only items of furniture were a small bed made from cast iron and a simple wooden bookcase, packed with volumes of various size and thickness.

At the foot of the bed sat a boy. He was perhaps ten years old, scrawny almost to the point of being skeletal, with a mop of ragged wild hair. At first glance, Sharpe thought him unremarkable, save for his eyes, which were the angry grey of a thundery ocean sky.

Sharpe closed the door in the master's peering face. His gaze returned to the child.

"Are you here to take me away?" said the boy.

Sharpe brushed a smudge from the silver handle of his cane. "That depends," he said, and he indicated the bookcase. "You like to read?"

The boy nodded. "I love it. The words let me go somewhere else in my head, away from here."

Vindictus Sharpe scanned the contents of the bookcase. There were some children's stories there, among them *Alice's Adventures in Wonderland* and *Treasure Island*. But there were also books that were not for children.

"You have read all of these?" he asked, tapping the complete works of Shakespeare with his cane.

The boy nodded.

The tall man bowed his head. "Impressive. Tell me: are you aware that the master is scared of you?"

The grey of the boy's eyes seemed to deepen and intensify. "Everyone's scared of me. And they should be."

"And why might that be?" asked Sharpe.

The boy fixed him with a cold stare. "Because," he said, "I can do things that they can't. I can do things that nobody can." He nodded towards the door. "They call me a monster."

Vindictus Sharpe's face remained as blank as the walls.

"Show me," he said.

The boy's gaze travelled to the bookcase. At once it began to tremble. Several books tumbled to the floor. And then one of the books, bound in green leather, shot away from the shelves as though it had been thrown. But this book did not hit the floor. Its pages opened and began to flap, and the book circled over Sharpe's head like an awkward bird.

After thirty seconds or so, the book thudded to the bare stone floor.

Sharpe's face remained calm, but the boy could see that something in his eyes had changed.

"Everything all right in there?" came the master's voice from out in the hallway. Neither the boy nor the tall man answered.

"Why aren't you scared of me?" asked the boy.

Sharpe said nothing. For the first time, the boy was aware of how strikingly blue his eyes were.

Without warning, every remaining book on the shelves soared into the air, and began to circle and swoop around the room, never colliding, though there were many of them.

The boy's mouth fell open. He watched and watched, until Sharpe glanced towards the bookcase, and in seconds the books were back, each in exactly the spot it had previously occupied.

Vindictus Sharpe flattened out a crease on one of his leather gloves. His blue eyes met the grey eyes of the boy.

"I am not afraid of you," he said, "because I am a monster too."

A doctor from the city asylum arrived at the orphanage early next morning. He had been called upon to evaluate one of the boys – a child who had been involved in unexplained and, occasionally, violent incidents. When the master led him down the narrow stairs to the dark corridor and opened the door, he was at a loss to explain where the boy might have gone, or why several of the books were missing from the bookcase.

The doors to the building were locked immediately, and every inch of the place searched. But there was no trace of the child. He had simply vanished.

The master had no recollection of ever having answered the door the previous night. He possessed no memory of Vindictus Sharpe in his impeccable suit, or how he had led him to the boy in the basement. He certainly could not remember how he himself had helped to pack the child's belongings and seen them safely out.

That night, and every night thereafter, the master would dream of a man and a boy walking together through the falling snow. Though he ran, he could never quite catch them up.

CHAPTER 5

THROUGH THE DOORS

Daniel's eyes cracked open a fraction. He screwed up his face at the sunlight flooding the room. He sat up, and rubbed his eyes with a knuckle. The blurred edges of his mind began to focus.

He lay in a small, comfortable bed in a cosy room with an arched wooden roof. At the opposite end of the room were two doors, one of which was open. Through the open door, Daniel could hear the sound of birdsong and the babbling whisper of running water. He shuffled to the edge of the bed, swung his legs from beneath the thick duvet. His bare feet sank into a deep carpet.

Memories came bursting back: of running through Glasgow, Spud chasing close behind; of the

36

horror as the car came towards him; of hitting the hard ground.

Daniel climbed from the bed and stumbled towards a small mirror that hung between the doors. He gazed at his reflection, expecting to see cuts and bruises, but there were no marks on him, no sign that he had been hurt at all. A great fear began to build in his chest. His lungs tightened. His head spun. What if … what if he had been hit by a car?

Am I dead?

He did not have time to contemplate this question, because a flicker of movement drew his attention to the window, and he realised that a girl was staring at him through the glass.

He stumbled backwards as she moved to the door. She stood in the doorway, brushing long wild curls from her grey eyes. She looked him up and down, arms crossed.

"Enjoy your snooze, did you?" she said. "Nice and comfy?" She looked around the room and shook her head. "Unbelievable. This is nicer than *my* room!"

"Who're you?" said Daniel. "Where am I? Am I … dead?"

The girl screwed up her face, took another step into the room.

"Dead? What are you going on about? Why would you be *dead?*"

Daniel blinked. "But … but I was standing right

in the middle of a busy road! A car was going to hit me…"

The girl tapped her foot on the floor. "He must have saved you. I wonder why. What's your name?"

"Daniel," said Daniel. "Who are you talking about? Who must have saved me?"

But the girl was already opening the blue door, the one that had been closed.

"This is all very strange," she said. "No one new ever shows up here." She narrowed her eyes. "Nobody real anyway. Stay put. I'm going to find out exactly what's going on."

And she slipped off through the blue door before Daniel could ask her name, or why she was so interested in him, or what she'd meant about nobody *real* ever showing up.

Daniel patted himself on the chest. He felt real. He certainly didn't feel dead. Then again, how would he know what being dead felt like? He stared at the door through which the girl had left, and tried the handle. The door was locked. So he went to the second door, the open one. A hilltop view lay before him, patchwork fields and a forest beyond, under a crystal blue sky. The air was warm and sweet as honey.

Daniel stepped down some narrow wooden stairs into a meadow of waist-high grass. He realised he'd been in a wooden caravan – the sort of wagon he imagined travelling folk might use, or circus performers in olden times. The wagon was painted a deep, shimmering blue, decorated with golden flourishes. Something struck him then: if this was all real, how could that girl possibly have left through a door *inside* the wagon?

He was thirsty; his tongue was sticking to the roof of his mouth. He moved towards the stream, bent down and drank. The water was ice cold and pure, and probably the best drink he'd ever had.

"Ah! Awake I see!"

At the sound of the voice, Daniel spat out a mouthful of water, spun, caught a fleeting glimpse of a dusty grey suit and then tripped over his own tangled feet, tumbling to the grass.

"Oh, very graceful," said the man in the suit. "The Royal Ballet will be knocking at the door any time now."

Daniel scrambled to his feet, rubbing his elbow, and recognised the owner of the Nowhere Emporium immediately. "You! What are *you* doing here? What am *I* doing here? Am I dreaming?"

The man in the dusty suit scratched his nose. His wild hair swayed in the breeze. "We're all dreaming, Daniel Holmes, in our own way. Follow me, if you will." At this he turned and marched up the wooden steps, into the wagon.

Daniel hurried after him.

"Wait! Where's the girl?" he asked, once they were inside.

"Girl?" the man said. "Don't bother yourself with her. You have more important things to think about at the moment." He opened the blue door and indicated the shadowy beyond. "This way. All will be explained."

Daniel took a slow step towards the door. He peered through.

"That's not right," he said. "That *can't* be right."

Beyond the blue door was a square entrance hall, like the inside of a castle, that seemed to climb up and up forever, criss-crossed with a hundred – or a thousand – entangled and intertwining stairways, all lit by the flickering glow of torchlight.

The man in the suit stepped into the hall. "Don't look so worried," he said. "Nothing can harm you in here. I checked the corridors yesterday, caught the last of the escaped lions."

He wheeled away and began to stride across the hall.

Daniel was unsure what to do. He watched the man in the suit, and then his eyes widened. "Lions?" he said. "Hey! Wait! Wait up!"

CHAPTER 6

A BARGAIN WITH LUCIEN SILVER

"Would you like a cup of tea?"

The man in the grey suit sat behind his desk, stirring tea in a china cup.

"No," said Daniel. He watched a small whirlpool form in the liquid and tried to sound braver than he felt. "No tea, thank you. Just tell me what's going on."

He had followed the man across the hallway, passing dozens of staircases, to another doorway – this one with a curtain of deep, red velvet. When he'd brushed through the curtain Daniel had found himself back in the Emporium.

The man in the suit sipped at his tea, then returned his cup to a saucer on the desk.

"There really is no way of making what I'm about

to say any easier for you to hear or comprehend," he began. "So here it is: Daniel Holmes, you should be dead." At this he stood, and began to wander around the shop, his hands clasped behind his back. "Allow me to explain. My name is Lucien Silver. I am a ... traveller. This Emporium is my means of transport. It dances through time, taking me from city to city, town to town, village to village, all over the globe."

"Through time?" said Daniel. "Like Doc Brown?"

Mr Silver gave him a blank look. "Who?"

"Doc Brown," said Daniel. "You know. Marty McFly. *Back to the Future?* It's an old movie I saw at the children's home. Doc and Marty have a time machine."

Mr Silver shrugged. "I do not get to the cinema much," he said. His grey eyes sparkled in the light of the fire. "And my Emporium is not just a time machine." He pointed to the red curtain. "Beyond that curtain, beyond the many staircases we have just passed, lie my Wonders. Think of the Emporium as being like a tree. The hall of staircases you just walked through – that is the trunk. Branching off it are the passageways, hundreds of them, where the Wonders lie. Wherever I visit, customers are drawn to this place. For a small fee, I allow them to step through the curtain and experience what it's like to fly among the endless stars, to taste the colour of the sunset and explore the very boundaries of imagination. I allow them to visit my Wonders.

"Of course, I cannot allow my customers to remember

what they have seen in the Emporium. Not any more. Many years ago, when the shop first opened, they remembered everything. But we soon became much too busy to cope with the crowds. Now they leave with a foggy glow of happiness, perhaps even the sense that their life has changed forever. But they cannot recall the shop. To them, it's as if it never existed."

He frowned, and a sudden weight seemed to cause him to sag. "When you ran away, strayed onto that road, you nearly died."

Daniel opened his mouth, but found his throat thick and choked.

"If that's true, if I nearly died, then why am I here? How did I get out alive?"

"Because I interfered," said Silver. "I saved you, Daniel. I don't know if it was the right thing to do. It was not an easy decision to make. But the day you returned to the Emporium – the moment I realised you remembered being here the previous day – I knew you were special. I knew there must be a reason why you came to my attention."

"What sort of reason?"

"I don't know yet," said Mr Silver, drumming his fingers on his chin. "But I am offering you the chance of a lifetime, my boy – the chance of a hundred lifetimes. Come with me. Learn about the Emporium. Prove that I was right to interfere. See the world in a way nobody else can. What do you say?"

Daniel said nothing. He stared out of the

Emporium's windows. Glasgow was hidden beneath a veil of thick swirling fog.

"You need persuasion," said Mr Silver. "Seeing is believing, or so they say."

He strode towards the shop door, reaching for an elaborate metal instrument on the wall. To Daniel, it looked like a complicated cross between a clock and a compass. There were many dials, and rings of numbers set within smaller rings. Mr Silver began to manipulate the hands of the instrument. When he was satisfied, he spun and headed for the fire, scooping a handful of coal from a bucket on the floor. He tossed the coal into the fire. There was a great roar, and the flames became so bright Daniel shielded his eyes. For the briefest moment, the flames burned a deep red, and the fire exploded, sending a plume of soot billowing into the store.

As Daniel coughed the soot from his lungs, a bar of bright sunlight began to burn through the smoke. When the soot had settled, Mr Silver stood by the door of the Emporium and opened it with a flourish.

"See for yourself," he said.

Daniel stepped to the doorway and felt a warm breeze on his face. He had been expecting, of course, to look out onto a Glasgow street; to see shoppers bustling past, weighed down with bags.

But that is not what he saw.

He inched out of the door onto a wide walkway. The air was warm, the sky awash with deep reds and purples. Beyond the walkway, where a road should surely have been, there was a canal lined with tall narrow buildings, all columns and spires and colourful shutters.

"What happened to Glasgow?" Daniel said, ducking back into the Emporium as a passing old woman, laden with a heavy basket, stopped and peered suspiciously at him.

Mr Silver shut the door and made sure the sign in the window read CLOSED.

"We left," he said, as though this was the most regular occurrence in the world. "That's Venice. We're in Venice now." He glanced at the instrument on the wall. "The year is 1854. July, I believe."

Daniel craned his neck to get a better view from the window. He wiped the glass, which was foggy from his breath. He tried to find some words.

"It's impossible!"

"Yet here we are," said Mr Silver.

Daniel felt the need to sit down. "So we're ... we're ... we've just ... this is ... really?"

"Indeed," said Silver.

"But. I mean. How? Just ... *how?*" Daniel's eyes widened. "It's magic, isn't it? It has to be! How else can we have just come from a caravan in a meadow that's *inside* a room? There's no other way for all of this to be real, to be happening."

Mr Silver smiled. "One thing at a time, Mr Holmes. One thing at a time."

"And you want me to come with you? All around the world?"

A pause.

Daniel narrowed his eyes. "What's the catch?"

"The catch, Daniel Holmes, is that you will work to earn your place here. What I am offering is not a holiday. It is an opportunity. A challenge. You must show me I was correct to bring you here, that you are, as I suspect, special. If you succeed in that, then the Emporium will become your home."

"And what happens if I don't come up to scratch?" said Daniel. "You sack me? Leave me somewhere halfway round the world a hundred years before I was born?"

"I will do no such thing," said Mr Silver. "If you do not belong in the Emporium, you will simply be returned to your own time. Your old life." He offered a hand. "So, do we have a bargain?"

Daniel organised the facts in his mind: he was an orphan leading a miserable life; he didn't have any friends; a gang of bullies had made it their mission to ensure his life was as uncomfortable as possible; he was lost.

And now he'd been invited to escape all of that and travel through time in a magical shop, with a man he suspected was either a genius or a lunatic – or maybe both. He had the opportunity to be someone else, even if it was just for a while. And if he was someone else, maybe he wouldn't feel so alone.

"I'll do it," he said.

CHAPTER 7

OPENING NIGHT

Next morning, as Daniel dressed, he stared out of his wagon at the blazing sun, low in the morning sky. He did not trust his own eyes. As far as Daniel could tell, his wagon and the meadow outside it were somehow contained *inside* a room *within* the shop. How did it all work? How did Mr Silver bring outside *inside*? Was it like a movie set? An illusion? If he were a bird flying in the sky above the wagon, would he get only so high and reach a wall?

The familiar sound of beating wings, and Mr Silver's gleaming magpies glided through the open door. They fluttered around his head, touched down on his shoulders, stamped their feet and pecked at him. They twitched their heads and flapped this way and that.

Get ready! No time to lose! they seemed to be telling him. Daniel finished getting dressed. The magpies chased him out of the door, across the hall of stairways and through the curtain.

Mr Silver was waiting behind his desk in the shop front.

"The only downside to travelling by flame," he said, expecting Daniel to know what he was talking about, "is the mess it tends to create." He ran his hand along a tabletop, coating his fingertips with a thick layer of soot. "Your official Emporium duties, in the beginning at least, will consist of keeping the front of shop presentable. I expect this place to be shining when we open to the public this evening."

Daniel gazed around the soot-covered room. "When do we open?"

Silver raised a finger, shook off the soot. "Our doors open at twilight and close at dawn."

And so, with excitement buzzing through him, and a job to keep his mind busy, Daniel set to work, cleaning and tidying and clearing the place of soot. Everything was filthy. How long had it been since Mr Silver last cleaned? Daniel adjusted columns of books and polished the silver and jet stone pieces of a beautiful chess set. Every time he turned away, the pieces would move around the board, as though a game between two invisible opponents was underway.

So much work made the day rush past, and by early

evening the day had melted to twilight. Daniel became aware that a curious crowd was beginning to gather outside. He peered out through the window.

"Why haven't they come before now?" he said. "We've been here for two days."

Mr Silver, who was at his desk writing in his battered old book, barely glanced up.

"Most of them haven't noticed us until now," he said.

Daniel narrowed his eyes.

"You mean you haven't let them notice, don't you?"

To which Mr Silver only smiled.

Then, at last, Silver snapped his book shut, locked it away in its drawer, stood up, and threw on his coat.

"Showtime," he said, patting his hair in a futile attempt to flatten the wild tangle.

The door of the Emporium creaked open. Silence poured into the shop, deep and electric. Daniel held his breath, listening to the drumbeat of his own heart.

Mr Silver held out his right hand, then waved his left hand over it. Where only a moment ago there had been nothing but empty space, a dove sat in his palm, white feathers glowing in the light of the fire. Daniel breathed a hundred different scents: chocolate and wood fire, pipe smoke and cinnamon. Mr Silver's grey eyes shone as he released the dove and watched it fly out into the darkness.

"Welcome to opening night, Daniel Holmes."

A flash of light illuminated the darkened sky.

Then the customers began to come.

Their eyes grew wide as they caught sight of the treasures within the Emporium. Grown men and women became like children once more, anxious to touch and inspect every shining trinket.

When they noticed the curtain, Mr Silver would pull back the material with a flourish, inviting them to witness the Wonders beyond. Daniel watched with fascination as they filtered through. His mind fizzed with curiosity.

"This is supposed to be a shop," he said. "So how come nobody's buying anything?"

Mr Silver wagged a finger.

"That, Daniel, is where you are wrong. Come with me."

The moment he stepped back through the curtain, Daniel knew something magical had happened. The entrance hall full of staircases, once steeped in shadow and silence, had become alive with warmth and light. The soft flicker of the torches had intensified, reflecting and dancing on the sparkling walls. Aromas of caramel and spice filled the air.

The hallways were dotted with performers and vendors, men and women scattered here and there, at the foot and summit of stairways. Each was dressed in a combination of black and shimmering gold. Some handed out candyfloss, or caramel apples, or warm chocolate pies; others performed magic tricks, or juggled, or swallowed swords. No two were identical.

"Where did they come from?" said Daniel, passing a bare-chested man who was breathing fire. The flames formed the shape of a pouncing tiger, then an elephant, and finally a dragon.

"From within," said Mr Silver.

As they walked, they passed several customers chattering excitedly about rooms that contained impossible things: oceans and deserts and windows to the stars. A little girl tugged on the sleeve of her mother's coat. "I saw a dragon, Mama!" she was saying. "A real dragon with fire breath and wings and a spiky black tail!"

"I can understand what they're saying!" said Daniel, who had until that moment forgotten that he was in a foreign country, and that these people were not speaking in English.

"Of course you can," said Silver. "What use would I have for an assistant who could not communicate with my customers? You can now understand and speak any language that you may need."

Daniel tried to remain cautious, suspicious even — mostly because nothing he cared about tended to hang around for very long. But wonder had begun to chip away at his armour.

"Are there other shops like this?" he asked. "Is there more magic out there?"

"There is nowhere else like my Emporium," Mr

Silver said. "There is magic, certainly, and plenty of it – but it exists at the edges of things, in the corner of the eye and the back of the mind. Our world is filled with the extraordinary, Daniel. For many reasons, most people only see the things they wish to see. They are afraid of anything that cannot be explained by a scientific formula or written in a textbook. So they ignore the unknown. But for those of us who open our eyes, those who truly dare to wonder, there is treasure everywhere."

They went around a sharp bend and through a tunnel of black stone to a door set in a corridor of black slate. A golden nameplate was attached to the centre of the door, and looping letters spelled out simply:

Mr Silver reached into his coat, producing a crimson scarf and gloves, pulling them on with great care. He opened the door.

The cold breath of winter brushed Daniel's face. He sucked in a deep lungful of air. It smelled like a December morning.

Mr Silver's feet crunched on the ground as he stepped through the door. Daniel followed, moving from dim hallway to clean sunlight. He was standing on a frozen pond in the middle of thick woodland. Everything around him glittered with a coating of frost, from the tips of the tallest trees to the forest floor.

In the centre of the pond stood a simple fountain made from three circular tiers of stone. A thin silvery liquid flowed over the stones.

Mr Silver smiled at the look on Daniel's face.

"You question whether my customers are actually buying anything? I can assure you that they are. I sell them amazement. I am a merchant of wonder." He leaned over and gathered a pile of frost from the frozen pond, rubbing it between his gloved fingers. "But my customers do not pay for their experience in the Emporium with coins or notes. No. My price is a piece of their imagination."

Daniel took one step back.

"Oh, it's easily done, if you know the way," Silver said. "Customers are free to wander through the doors, to be amazed and wonderstruck." He indicated the silver solution that flowed over the fountain. "The Emporium takes a little of their brimming wonder, their imagination – never enough for the customer to miss it of course – and it becomes the liquid you see here. It is the fuel that powers everything you see; the lifeblood of the Emporium. Imagination is the root of magic."

"Do they know?" said Daniel. In the pit of his stomach he felt sick at the thought of imagination being extracted from clueless customers. "Do you tell people what you're doing to them?"

Silver shook his head. For a fleeting moment he looked old and fragile, standing in the frost.

"It wasn't always this way. There was a time, when I was a younger man, that my own imagination was enough. But I am growing older. I must keep the Emporium running. And no harm comes to anyone – that is a promise! Imagination is alive. It grows in the mind like a tree. The Emporium merely clips a few of the branches. What little I take grows back, in time." He observed Daniel. "If this has changed things, if you wish to leave, you may do so. I will drop you back in your own time. Just say the word."

Daniel stared at the fountain, at the silvery imagination flowing over the stone.

He was filled with doubts and questions, and he was wary of Mr Silver's power. He considered what it might be like to return to his life, to the rain-soaked streets of Glasgow; to loneliness, and to nobody. He looked into Mr Silver's serious grey eyes.

"I don't want to go back," he said. "I want to stay, and see the world. I want to learn about magic. I want to know secrets. I want to be somebody."

A smile played on Silver's lips, and he bowed his head to Daniel. "As you wish."

Something moved in the tops of the trees, a blinding flash of silver soaring into the blue sky.

"How did you do it?" Daniel asked. "How do you make all of this?"

"Tomorrow," said Mr Silver. "Tomorrow I will start your lessons. And we will begin to find out if you have what it takes to become a part of the Nowhere Emporium. Tomorrow, the first test awaits!"

"What sort of test?"

But no answer came.

Daniel stood alone in the frozen world. The only sign that Mr Silver had been in the woodland at all was a trail of footprints in the frost.

CHAPTER 8

A NEW PROJECT

Edinburgh, January 1883

The carriage pulled up outside a row of townhouses, wheels skidding on the snow-packed street. Steam rose from two slick black horses as the coachman leapt from his seat and opened the carriage door.

A pair of passengers stepped down onto the frozen ground.

First was Vindictus Sharpe. His striking blue eyes and neat silver hair and goatee flashed in the light of the snow-white city as he glanced around the familiar skyline running up the slope of the old town to Edinburgh Castle. Close on Sharpe's heels was a young man, perhaps fifteen years of age. He was short and slight, dressed in a dusty grey pinstripe suit, messy waves of hair falling over a face halfway to becoming handsome.

Vindictus Sharpe paid the coachman without tipping him, and led his young companion up a slippery stone staircase. He rapped three times on the townhouse door with the silver handle of his cane.

The door opened almost immediately.

"How may I help you?" said the butler of the house.

"We are here to see Ms Birdie Sandford," said Sharpe. "She is not expecting us, but I am sure she will not turn down the opportunity to catch up with an old friend."

The butler looked at the pair for a moment. "Who should I say is calling?"

"Vindictus Sharpe. She will recognise the name. We shared the stage together for a while."

The butler nodded. "Very well. Please wait here."

The door closed. A light flurry of snow began to fall. Man and boy stood in silence.

A few minutes later, the door was opened by a tiny old woman with a beehive of silver hair. Her eyes, magnified by thick lenses, looked Sharpe up and down.

"Vindictus Sharpe? What has it been? Twenty years? My God! You haven't aged a day."

Sharpe bowed his head. "And neither have you, Birdie."

"I thought you were a better liar than that," she said with a dismissive wave. "Come in out of the snow."

They followed her into the house, which was spacious and grand, and smelled of flowery perfume. She led them to a large sitting room on the second floor, where the butler was waiting. He poured a brandy for Birdie, a whisky for Sharpe, a cup of hot tea for the young man, and then left the room, closing the doors.

Birdie sipped from her glass, sucking air through her teeth as the liquor burned her throat.

"I will spare you the usual pleasantries," she said. "I know you find them as tiresome as I do. We will come straight to the point: I assume you have resurfaced after these many years because you have a business proposition?"

Sharpe leaned forward in his chair. He sipped from his glass. "I do indeed. Do you recall why I decided to take a break from performing in our magic shows?"

Birdie sipped her brandy. "Of course," she said. "You wished to dabble in teaching, which I found strange considering your dislike for children. Is your daughter still locked away in that school?"

Sharpe waved the question away.

"I am not merely dabbling. Twenty years ago, in Frankfurt, a hag visited my dressing room. She told me that one day I would find a pupil, and that together we would push magic to places it has never been."

Birdie indicated the young man with her mahogany walking stick. "Is the boy good?"

Sharpe laughed. "Good? He has the potential to be great – almost as great as me. I believe we could sell out theatres across the world. That is why I have come. If I'm training the boy to change the world, then the least we can expect is to make a little money along the way, don't you think?"

Birdie's eyes turned to the young man, who looked at his feet. "Are you interested in taking to the stage, boy?"

"Yes ma'am. Mr Sharpe has been preparing me."

"Would you care to show me?"

The boy glanced at Sharpe, who had instructed him that he should never, under any circumstances, admit to his talents in public. He had no wish to upset his teacher; a great many beatings had taught him his place, and knocked impeccable manners into him.

"It's acceptable in these circumstances," Sharpe said. "Birdie is aware of our abilities. She has considerable connections in the world of entertainment, and she has made a great deal of money, thanks to me."

"And you thanks to me," said Birdie with a prim smile. "Show me what you can do, boy."

The young magician breathed deeply. He concentrated on the tendrils of steam rising from the cup of tea in his hands. Immediately, the steam began to flow faster, gathering together in smooth curls near the boy's feet and pushing upward. Forming at first the sketchy outline of a man, the steam refined, rough edges smoothing to become a work of art – until a replica of Birdie's butler stood in the centre of the room. The steam butler walked silently towards Birdie, bowing before her, planting a kiss on her hand. Then the figure spun in a circle, coat-tails flying, and vanished, leaving only a misty silhouette fading slowly to nothing.

Birdie stared at the air where the steam had been, her mouth open. At last, she turned to Vindictus Sharpe, a wide smile breaking across her face.

"What do you have in mind?" she asked.

CHAPTER 9

THE BOOK OF WONDERS

The nightmare never changed: Daniel was trapped in a sinking fishing boat. He could hear the calls of his father as he groped around in the darkness, but he couldn't find him, couldn't do anything to help. He woke with a desperate gasp just as the freezing water closed over his head.

A silver magpie with sparkling ruby eyes sat on the pillow beside him. Its twin was hopping around the foot of the bed. The magpie had dropped a small black envelope onto Daniel's pillow. It nudged the envelope towards him until the sharp paper pressed against his nose. Inside he found a black card with a message in golden ink.

Your first lesson shall commence in one hour.
Follow the magpies.

Mr S

Daniel turned the card over in his hands, still trembling from the bad dream. What sort of lesson lay in wait?

In the wagon he found a wardrobe filled with black trousers and sweaters, crisp white shirts and golden ties – his Emporium uniform.

"Go on then," he said to the magpies when he was dressed. The birds fluttered through Daniel's bedroom door to the great hall of staircases. They began to climb through the Emporium, navigating the tangle of steps in a series of swoops and spins and slows. As he followed the birds from one staircase to another, higher and higher, Daniel glimpsed many corridors of shining black brick. Countless doors lay along those passageways. But what lay beyond the doors? *Wonders*, Mr Silver had called them.

Somewhere along the way Daniel spotted movement in the shadows and realised that the girl he'd seen in his wagon was watching him. He took a step towards her and raised his hand, but she hurried away into the darkness like a startled fox and was gone. He would have to ask Mr Silver about her. Perhaps after his lesson.

One of the magpies pecked his ear, letting him know that it was not amused by the disruption, and they were moving again, until finally the birds landed at the foot of a wide door. Daniel pulled it open.

The walls of the square room beyond were completely hidden under rows of bookcases. He narrowed his eyes, squinting at the walls, and realised upon closer inspection that there were, in fact, no bookcases. There were only books. The books *were* the walls. And in that moment it hit him: every object in the room, from the armchairs to the tables to the lamps, was made from books, or the covers of books, or pages that had been torn from books. The floor was made of books. The ceiling was made of books. A miraculous fire was burning in a fireplace made entirely of books.

"Glad you could make it."

There were two armchairs. Both had been empty when Daniel walked into the room. He was sure of it. Now, somehow, Mr Silver occupied one of them. He nodded to Daniel, motioned for him to sit opposite.

"Let us begin at the beginning," said Mr Silver, wasting no time. "First, the basics. I deal in awe and wonderment. I sell escape and fantasy. I give my customers a tantalising glimpse of all that is possible in this world. And though they cannot remember the shop upon leaving, they will find that their hearts are lighter, that the edges of the world are bright and new and shining. In return, the Emporium takes a piece of imagination, and that imagination powers the place, allowing me to create new Wonders and travel to my next destination, where the process begins anew." He ran his hands through his wild brown hair, and for a moment the shadow of age passed over his face.

"Magic can help one accomplish incredible things, Daniel. Take time, for instance. If you know enough, you can do things with time you wouldn't believe. I once worked for a man who never aged. Not one day the whole time I knew him." Silver shook his head, and his eyes darkened. "He's still out there somewhere, probably looking exactly as he did when I last saw him. I myself managed to stop the clock a few years after we parted ways, though I use a different method. I didn't have the stomach for his." Daniel wondered what the man who never aged had done, exactly. But Mr Silver waved a hand, as though flicking away the memories.

"The point is, I am older than I seem, and I'm beginning to feel the weight of the Emporium upon my shoulders. This is why I have decided to take on an assistant." He nodded to Daniel. "Do you recall what I was doing when you first found the shop?"

"I think," said Daniel, screwing up his eyes as he tried to replay the memory in his head, "you were writing. At your desk."

Silver reached into the pocket of his coat. He placed the battered old book on his lap. "I was writing in this book," said Silver. He took it up and fanned the pages, causing his wild hair to blow into his eyes. "And *what* a book. It is the key to this place. The secret behind the Emporium. My *Book of Wonders*."

Daniel stared at the cracked cover. The title was all but faded away, though there were places where gold lettering was still visible; he could decipher the letters L, S, W, O and D. He leaned in. Was it his imagination, or could he feel the book pulling at him, drawing him closer?

Silver continued. "For every room that will ever come to exist in the Emporium, there is a page in this book. When I have an idea for a new Wonder, and I've thought it through carefully and decided that it is suitable, I begin to write it down. The pages are enchanted and entwined with the shop. When I have finished writing, a Wonder will appear somewhere in the corridors."

"All the doors I saw on the way here?" said Daniel. "All the Wonders? They have a page in that book?"

Silver thumbed through the pages, selecting one passage and placing the open book on the table. The writing within, in deep black ink, was small and neat, and decorated with many curls and flourishes. There was also a sketch, drawn in flowing black lines that seemed to come alive as Daniel gazed at it.

"I recognise this," he said, leaning ever closer to the book. "It's my wagon!"

Silver smiled for a fleeting moment, causing the lines around his eyes to deepen.

"Correct," he said. "I trust you find it comfortable enough? If you wish me to change anything…"

"It's perfect," said Daniel. His fingers fluttered hungrily, and he felt a great rush of excitement as he asked, "Can I have a closer look?"

A hesitation.

Silver handed over the book.

It was heavier than Daniel expected. But it also felt familiar somehow, as if he had held it before. He flicked through page after page, noting in his mind a list of rooms he longed to visit. There was an underground lake of gold, and a cove filled with sapphire water where a mermaid whispered the whereabouts of buried treasure. He saw a path through an enchanted forest, and the mountaintop den of an armour-clad dragon, and a grassland populated by lions. There were ancient pages where the ink was worn and could not be properly read. One such passage caught his attention, and as he stared at the words his stomach told him that they contained something vast and dark and ancient.

"The Library of Souls," said Mr Silver. "I am a fan of stories. A collector. And there is no greater story than that of life. The Library of Souls holds on its many shelves the life story of everyone who has ever lived, everyone who *will* ever live."

Wonderstruck, Daniel tried to imagine a room vast enough to hold such a great number of books, but he was distracted when Mr Silver gasped and breathed through his teeth. He sat forward in his chair and held his hand to his chest.

"What's wrong?"

Silver closed his eyes tight and took a deep breath. He let the breath out slowly, opened his eyes, and blinked. "I'm fine," he said.

Daniel's eyes lingered on Silver's hand, which was still pressed to his chest.

"Now that you've seen inside the *Book of Wonders*," said Mr Silver, as if nothing had happened, "it is time for the first test." He held out an open hand. In his palm sat a golden fountain pen. Daniel stared at it.

"I don't understand."

"I want you to attempt a Wonder of your own. Write in the book."

"Me? Make a room appear from nowhere? You're having a laugh!"

"I certainly am not. It's the quickest way to judge whether you have any talent."

Daniel fidgeted in his chair. He had not imagined his first test could be something so huge. He took the pen from Silver.

"What if nothing happens?" he asked. "Will you sack me?" Now that he was holding the book, that he'd seen the Wonders within its pages, his old life seemed so very far away. It was like he'd been living in black and white, and suddenly the world was alive with colour and possibilities. He was not ready to return to the grey.

Silver thought about the question. "We shall worry about that if it happens." He mimed writing. "On you go."

Daniel found a blank page. His palms were wet.

"What should I write?"

"That is up to you," said Silver. "Though I would advise starting with something small. A solitary room, perhaps. Nothing too fancy."

Daniel thought and thought. Then, from nowhere, an image appeared in his mind, something comforting from his past, and the idea began to blossom and flower. When he was as certain as he could be, he began to write in Mr Silver's book.

When he had finished, the entire page was filled with the neatest handwriting he could manage. His fingers tingled warmly.

Silver motioned for Daniel to hand the book over.

"Do you think it worked?" Daniel's heart punched at the inside of his chest.

Mr Silver shook the messy hair from his eyes and went to the door.

"Let's find out," he said.

The Emporium was closed, which meant the corridors were deserted and cloaked in shadow. As he followed Silver, sticking close, Daniel imagined that he could hear the walls breathing. A shiver danced down his spine.

As if reading his mind, Mr Silver said, "It's perfectly safe to walk the corridors – to explore. In fact, I encourage it. Everything you see is under my control. Nothing will harm you. In all the years I have been welcoming customers into the Emporium, no one has left with so much as a bruise."

"It's just the thought of getting lost," said Daniel. "I could wander around forever."

"You will find your feet," said Silver. "Walking the corridors and passageways will become second nature. And know this: if, by some curious twist of fate, you find yourself in trouble, the Emporium will help you. All you have to do is ask."

Silver slowed at last. He tilted his head to the side, as if he were listening for some faraway sound. He took four slow steps, to the nearest shining black door, and pressed his ear against the surface. He stepped back. His gaze flicked from the door to Daniel and back.

"This is new," he said. "And it is not one of mine." He gave Daniel a curious look, like he was staring at some alien creature. "Open it."

Daniel trembled as he approached the door. Even after everything he'd seen these past few days, he couldn't quite believe that a new room had appeared simply because he'd written in an old book. And at the same time, he felt a strange sense of wondrous pride. But was it enough? Would he pass the test?

His hand was slick with sweat as it grasped the door handle. The lock gave a satisfying click. The door opened.

The room was circular and dim and cold, and in the centre stood a column of stone, honeycombed with hundreds, thousands, of open compartments. In each compartment sat a glass sphere. A staircase wound up around the column, stretching into endless darkness.

Mr Silver stared around. His mouth hung open a little.

Daniel reached out to touch the column. He half expected his hand to pass through, that it was not real. But his fingers found the cool, rough stone.

"It's real!" he whispered. "It's really here, just like I imagined when I was writing in the book!"

Silver selected a sphere from the column and spun it in his hands, watching as a flurry of snow whipped around the inside of the glass.

"Snow globes," he said. "Why snow globes?"

Daniel had already begun to climb the spiral staircase, staring at the hundreds of shining glass globes. Some were smaller than marbles, others larger than his head. Each was empty, save for the snowflakes inside.

"My mum collected them," Daniel said. "It's one of the only things I really remember about her from before Dad died. Before she was sad all the time.

When I was little, I'd sit on her knee and she'd tell me each one had a secret inside. That's what this room is: a place to keep secrets. The globes are empty because they're waiting to be filled. Whisper your secret into one and it'll be safe."

Mr Silver brushed his hands against a few of the snow globes. He stared about, a delighted twinkle dancing in his grey eyes.

"It is perfect for the Emporium," he said. Then he gazed up at the column of secrets, and smiled. "May I have the honour of leaving the first secret?"

Daniel felt a rush of pride.

"Go right ahead," he said. Leaving a secret was a very personal thing, so he turned away while Mr Silver climbed further up the steps and searched for the perfect globe.

When he reappeared, Daniel asked, "Did it work?"

A pause.

"I feel lighter," said Silver.

"I think that means it worked. So ... did I pass the test?"

Mr Silver seemed to be amused by the question. "You have talent," he said.

Daniel could not hide his proud smile. He felt giddy and important.

Mr Silver's face became very serious. He went on, "The *Book of Wonders* is a very powerful thing, Daniel. It is tied to me, entwined with my soul —

so entwined that we are almost one and the same. Your connection to the book is something new, and unexpected. If, by some tiny chance, you ever come across the book when you are alone, I must ask that you do not write a single word in its pages without me. You are inexperienced, raw; the results would be unpredictable. Dangerous even. Understand?"

"I mustn't write in the book without you," said Daniel.

Silver smiled, and bounded down the steps two at a time.

"From now on, you will write one page in the book every night after closing time. If you continue to show skill, I think there is much I can teach you. But be on your toes; at some point I will test you again, and I promise you will not see it coming."

Then he was gone, leaving Daniel alone with his secrets.

CHAPTER 10

THE GIRL AT THE DOOR

Mr Silver was true to his word — he allowed Daniel to write one page in the *Book of Wonders* each night — and soon Daniel's mind was overflowing with ideas and possibilities. He dreamt up plans for new Wonders as he cleaned the shop, and he followed customers as they entered the labyrinth of corridors, watching and learning all the time. He was determined to show Silver that his first attempt had not been a fluke. His connection to the book remained strong, and Mr Silver seemed impressed and delighted as each new Wonder appeared — though he tried to hide his excitement, rarely giving any compliment other than, "It will do."

Daniel also formed a routine to ease the fear of his

dreams. Whenever he woke from a nightmare, he'd climb from bed, walk to the shop front and gaze at the stars above Venice. The stillness of the city and the beauty of the night sky comforted him.

One night, as he stepped through the red velvet curtain, a cool breeze blew in from the canals. The shop door was already open.

Daniel recognised the girl at the door right away; she was the first person he'd seen when he woke up in his room in the Emporium. She stood in the doorway, curls of hair swaying in the breeze as she gazed out at the city on water, oblivious to Daniel's presence.

He watched her curiously. She was gripping the doorframe so tightly that her knuckles had turned white as bone. Her whole body seemed to shake as she lifted one foot from the floor and tried to step forward, out of the shop. She gasped and became breathless, straining as though she were struggling against something very powerful. Then she pulled her foot back and slumped against the doorframe. She began sobbing into her hands.

Daniel shifted from foot to foot. He was not very good with girls. Girls who cried were well out of his range of experience.

"Are you all right?" he asked, because it was the only thing that came to mind.

The girl jumped at the sound of his voice. She

shot him a look so sharp it could have burst a balloon.

"Do I look all right to you?" she said, rubbing her eyes.

"Well…" Daniel fumbled with the words. "Is there anything I can do?"

The girl shook her head. "You? There's nothing you can do." She sniffed, and narrowed her eyes. "What are you playing at anyway … spying on me?"

Oh, no … it wasn't like that," said Daniel. "I wasn't spying." A thought occurred to him. "Anyway, you're one to talk about spying; when I first woke up you were peering through a window into my room!"

"That was different," said the girl with a shrug. "This is my home. I was making sure you weren't a murderer or something."

"Why didn't you come back?" said Daniel.

Another shrug. "Papa told me to keep away. He said I'm a bad influence, and he doesn't want anybody distracting you."

"Papa? Mr Silver? Is he your dad?"

"Yup. I'm Ellie." A mischievous smile spread across her face. "I'm a huge disappointment. I mean, he loves me to bits, I know that, but Papa wanted me to follow in his footsteps." She put on a deep voice, an impression of her father. "'Take over the business. Keep it in the family.' But there isn't a magic bone in my body. I'm useless. So he's been banging on about finding an assistant." She frowned. "I never thought he'd actually go through with it. He's never invited anyone behind the scenes before. But here you are." She looked him up and down. "How can a person be so skinny? You look like you'd blow over in a breeze."

Daniel patted his stomach. "Not that skinny," he mumbled.

"What's he got you doing, anyway?"

"Cleaning, mostly," said Daniel.

Ellie wrinkled her nose. "You're a skivvy? Doesn't sound like much fun. Have you seen many of Papa's Wonders? The Circus of Bones? The Waterfall? What about the Fountain? Oh, I love the Fountain! Funny to think all that pretty watery stuff is actually imagination, isn't it? The Emporium takes it from the customers, uses it like ... like petrol in a car, I suppose. Papa's very clever."

"Yeah, I've seen one or two," said Daniel, skipping over the fact that he had actually created a number of his own. He didn't think Ellie would think much of that. He'd seem like a teacher's pet.

"Of course," said Ellie, "Papa used to be able to power all of it on his own. But he's getting older, you see. Well, not really older. Time does weird things in the Emporium. Papa hasn't aged at all for years." Her eyes sparkled. "The Wonders make life bearable around here. I'll show you my favourite." And she began to pull him by the arm towards the red velvet curtain.

"I thought Mr Silver told you to keep away from me."

"Technically," said Ellie, "you're the one who found me. So I'm not breaking any rules. Plus, he knows I'll get to you in the end."

Back through the curtain, up and up and up they went, staircase after staircase.

"You know what's weird?" said Daniel.

Ellie looked at him sideways. "You?"

"Apart from me," said Daniel. "I feel like I know where we're going. I mean, it's as if I know how to get anywhere inside the Emporium."

"Yup. The place gets under your skin."

Ellie's favourite door was located high in the Emporium, in a passageway with a polished floor made from black slabs of glass.

"Can't you even give me a clue what's inside?" said Daniel.

"And spoil the surprise? Never. Not knowing what's coming is part of the magic. It's a sort of test, I suppose."

"I've had enough tests," said Daniel. But it occurred to him then that perhaps Ellie was presenting him with the second test Mr Silver had mentioned – the one he wouldn't see coming.

"You'll like this one, I promise."

She halted, and indicated the arched door ahead. Daniel shifted forward and inspected a golden sign, engraved with the following words:

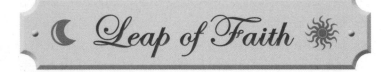

The chamber beyond was in complete darkness. Daniel took a slow step back.

"Don't be shy," she said, twisting a lock of hair around her finger. "Look, if we're going to get along, you'd better get used to having a little fun."

"I like having fun," said Daniel, edging towards the doorway. He pointed into the blackness. "I'm just not sure this looks fun."

"I'll go first," Ellie said. "I've done it a thousand times. Ready?"

Before Daniel could say anything else, Ellie grabbed him tight, wrapping her arms around his waist, and pulled him over the edge.

He was falling. Falling so fast, with the wind tearing into his face and his eyes and his ears, that he couldn't breathe. Ellie was no longer holding him. He shut his eyes tight, waiting for the moment when he'd smash into the ground.

It did not come.

When he opened his eyes, the world around him came to life.

Glimmering points of light erupted in the blackness, illuminating the heavens. Some were arranged in familiar constellations, others scattered like spilled diamonds.

Daniel realised that he was no longer frightened.

And he was no longer falling.

He let out a whoop of delight, the cool night air whipping through his hair as he flew, free as an eagle, through the night sky.

"Told you!" Ellie called as she tore past.

They lost sense of time as they flew, through fluffy clouds and falling snow in the crystal sky, until at last Ellie turned to him. "Head for the moon," she shouted. "I'll race you!"

Daniel did as she asked. The stars began to disappear, and the moon shifted and warped, becoming the familiar arch of a doorway.

They stepped from the sky onto the solid Emporium floor.

"So?" said Ellie, hopping on the spot. "What do you think?"

Daniel smiled at her enthusiasm.

"It's magic," he said.

"Of course it's magic," she said. "Magic is what Papa does best."

Daniel glanced back at the Leap of Faith doorway

as she led him away.

"How can one person do all of this?"

"Hmm?"

"Mr Silver. There are hundreds of doorways, thousands even. How has he had time to do it all?"

Ellie smirked.

"Like I said, time does funny things. Papa's been around for a while."

"You mean he's old? Older than he looks?"

"Much older. He's very, very old."

A staircase rumbled and shifted as they climbed it.

"Another thing," said Daniel. "When the shop is open, you can't turn a corner without bumping into a fire-breather or a juggler or something. Where are they now? Where do they go when we shut?"

"Come on," said Ellie. "I'll show you."

Five minutes later they were at another door, with a sign that read:

Through they went, stepping into a revolving glass door, which deposited them in a grand, open room with pillars of black marble and a sweeping staircase. The black carpet was deep and soft. At the far end of the room, between two golden elevators, was a service desk.

Daniel had never stayed in a hotel, but he had seen them in movies and magazines, and this place seemed at least as posh as the places Hollywood stars liked to stay.

"This is the Nowhere Hotel," said Ellie. "Every member of staff has a room here."

"It's not bad, is it?" said Daniel. "So how come I've never seen any of them coming and going from the shop? Don't they go outside?"

Ellie brushed her curls from her eyes, a gesture identical to her father's. "Hasn't Papa told you anything? The performers can't leave. They can't go past the red curtain. It's like a border, where the real world begins. They don't exist out there. To them, the Emporium *is* the world."

"But where did they come from?" asked Daniel. And then he raised a finger as the answer came to him. "Mr Silver wrote them all into his book, didn't he? They've popped out of the pages, just like his Wonders…" He trailed off when he saw Ellie's eyes growing wide.

"You know about Papa's book?"

"Em … yeah. He showed me."

"He must really like you. He never told me about the book till I was nine! And since I'm no good at writing in it, I'm not allowed to touch it. He thinks I'll lose it or something."

Daniel decided to change the subject. "So where do you stay?" he asked.

"Here. I've got a room in the hotel. Used to live in

Papa's private rooms with him but ... well, we don't always get along. He's a good man. I love him, really I do. But he's just so obsessed with the Emporium. I like it here, in the hotel. It's my own space."

"It's just you and your dad?" said Daniel.

"Yup."

"Where's your mum?"

"Who knows?" Ellie said. "Papa says I was about a week old when she left me on the doorstep of the Emporium. She never came back. Not once."

Daniel shook his head. "You know much about her?"

"Not really. I mean I've asked, obviously. Papa says I look like her. But I don't know why she left me here, or why she didn't want me. And I've sort of given up asking because Papa doesn't like to talk about it, and I don't like making him sad. I think he still loves her, even after all this time." She was silent for a moment, staring straight ahead. Then she blinked and said, "What about you? Where are your parents?"

"I'm an orphan," said Daniel. "Dad was a fisherman. Died at sea when I was four. Mum never got over that. We moved to Glasgow and she died two years later. I can't really remember much about them now. You know, real stuff, like how their voices sounded, or what their clothes smelled like ... It's like waking up and trying to remember a dream. It's there, but only for a second, and then it's gone again."

Ellie gave him a sad smile.

"This really is a nice place," he said, pointing around the lobby. "But it must be strange for the staff, knowing there's a whole world outside the Emporium and not being able to see it. It'd drive me mad!"

The colour drained from Ellie's face. "You don't miss what you've never had. That's what Papa says." Something had changed in her voice.

"But can you imagine?" said Daniel. "Not being able to experience all of the amazing places the Nowhere Emporium visits? We're lucky. We can see New York, and Cairo, and Paris ... watch kings and queens and governments come and go. We get to see everything, Ellie ... the whole of history—"

For a moment, Daniel thought she was going to reach over and slap him. But she closed her eyes, bit her lip and said, "I don't feel very well. I need some air."

She got up and rushed off across the lobby to the revolving door.

Confused and hurt, Daniel watched her for a moment, unsure what he'd done or what he should do. Eventually, he went after her, rushing across the lobby and through the revolving door, which spat him back out into the dark, sparkling corridors of the Emporium, right into the path of something that hit him like a train. Daniel slammed into the hard floor with a slap. He stared up at the concerned face of a huge bald man with a thick neck; and then up further still into the eyes of an enormously tall woman with dark brown skin, who wore an amused look – and a live yellow snake around her neck.

"Don't just stand there, Caleb. Help the boy up."

The man offered an enormous hand, which swallowed Daniel's hand, and pulled him to his feet.

"Sorry," Daniel said. "I should have been watching where I was going."

"What's the big rush?" asked Caleb. The huge bald man was wearing baggy black trousers and a black waistcoat with gold piping, unbuttoned to reveal a beer belly and chest covered in black hair. In his hands, which were the size of frying pans, he held a scruffy, dusty old teddy bear with no eyes.

"I know you," said Daniel. "You're the fire-breather, aren't you? The one who turns flames into animals?"

"Caleb, at your service," said the man. He jerked a fat thumb towards the impossibly tall woman. "This is Anja."

Anja nodded.

Caleb held out the stuffed bear. "And this is Mr Bobo."

Daniel stared at it. Caleb raised his eyebrows expectantly.

"Um ... Hello, Mr Bobo."

Caleb smiled. He said, "I found him many years ago, lying on the floor of one of the corridors. A child from the real world must have dropped him." He cradled the bear in his arms like a baby, proud and delighted that he owned something from the world beyond the Emporium.

"Caleb likes to collect things that the customers leave behind," said Anja. "He has built up a small collection of curiosities over the years."

Caleb rummaged in his pockets. He thrust his hand towards Daniel, and opened it. In his palm lay a half-sucked lemon sherbet, coated in grey fuzz. "I picked it up a month or two back. Would you like it? It might remind you of home."

"I'm fine," said Daniel, trying not to sound too disgusted. "But thanks."

"We know all about you, you know," said Anja. "Lucien Silver has an apprentice! It's the talk of the place. If you ask me, it's about time he got himself some help. How are you settling in?"

"Fine, I think," said Daniel. He craned his neck around them to stare down the passage. "Has Ellie passed this way?"

Anja's brow wrinkled. "We haven't seen her. Is something the matter?"

Daniel explained how Ellie had stormed off.

Caleb jutted out his bottom lip and nodded. "Ah. That would explain it."

"What? Explain what?"

"My guess," began Anja, patting her tightly curled black hair into place, "is that Ellie became angry because you were talking about how you are free to discover the world outside the Emporium's walls."

Daniel's mouth pursed. "But why would that make her mad?"

Caleb placed a heavy hand on Daniel's shoulder. "Because she's in the same boat as the staff," he said. "She can't leave the Emporium."

"What? How come?"

"We don't know the ins and outs of it," said Anja. "It's private business, after all. Ellie doesn't like to talk about it. But she's a lonely girl. You know, Daniel, you must be the first person from outside the Emporium to talk to Ellie in ... well, goodness knows how long."

"Really? What about the customers? She must talk to them, surely?"

Caleb shook his big head. "No. They can't see her or hear her. Something in the magic of this place has made Ellie invisible to anyone who isn't a part of the Nowhere Emporium. To most of the world, Daniel, Ellie Silver is nothing more than a ghost."

CHAPTER 11

BLADE OF FIRE

Next morning, the view from the shop window was very different to what Daniel had grown used to. There were no canals, no colourful shutters. Instead, there was a narrow cobbled lane, lined with unbroken rows of skinny houses and shops, and scattered with stalls selling a great number of different things. Mr Silver explained that they were now in Paris. He invited Daniel to walk the streets with him. Daniel, who had not left the shop since his arrival, jumped at the chance.

As they walked through the crowded backstreets, Daniel raised the subject of Ellie.

"I told her to keep away from you until you've had time to settle in!" said Silver with a resigned sigh. "Was she rude to you? She has a habit of being rude."

"She wasn't rude. I like her. She showed me around, and let me see her favourite Wonder."

Silver gave Daniel a sideward glance. "She has a favourite?"

"Yup. The Leap of Faith."

As they walked, Daniel became aware that Mr Silver was, undoubtedly, disguising a limp. His right leg seemed stiff, and he gritted his teeth when his weight shifted to that side.

"Do you mind me asking … is it true Ellie can't leave the shop?" said Daniel.

Silver seemed caught off guard by the question. "She has a condition that prevents her from going outside," he said. He did not elaborate.

"What sort of condition?" asked Daniel. "A disease? What'll happen if she does go out?"

Silver grimaced. He rubbed his leg. "Look, Ellie is safe in the Emporium. That is all you need to know."

"And is it true that the customers can't see her?"

Silver gave him an irritated look. "Yes."

"And that's part of this condition as well?"

Silver nodded, and grimaced again. "No more of this," he said. "We are not here to discuss Ellie."

"Of course not," said Daniel, and he knew not to push too far. "Why are we here?"

"Looking for something," said Silver. "I'll know it when I see it."

"Is your leg all right?"

"Fine."

On they walked. Daniel soon realised they were not out for a leisurely stroll around the sightseeing spots of Paris. They stuck to the backstreets and alleys, visiting several shops and stalls in the darkest corners of the city, each connected to the elusive and shadowy world of magic. There was a shop whose owner claimed to be in possession of a magic carpet, a stall selling the blood of many different animals, and an old woman who sold potions and powders from a flat overflowing with rats. None of these places, though, seemed to sell what Mr Silver wanted, and each failure only darkened his mood.

"These are the places you were talking about, aren't they?" said Daniel, breaking the silence as they approached another winding lane. "The magic places normal people can't see – or choose not to?"

Silver gave a nod. His limp had subsided a little, but Daniel could tell that he was still in pain.

"What exactly are we looking for?"

"Treasure."

It occurred to Daniel that Silver must be ill. Was he looking for some sort of medicine?

An apothecary sat at the end of the lane, leaning at a strange angle, as if it had been propped up by something that had suddenly disappeared. In the window, Daniel saw many dust-smothered bottles and jars, arranged around a human skeleton. He hoped it wasn't real.

The interior of the apothecary was filled with a silvery fog that stuck in Daniel's throat. A sharp metallic smell hung all around. Mr Silver purchased several items, among them a glass jar of black powder and a strangely shaped bottle filled with red liquid. But none of them seemed to be the mysterious item that he was so desperate to find, and by the time they left, Silver's mood had become quite black.

Daniel did not speak as he hurried along after him. He did not dare. In a mood like this, the air around Silver seemed to crackle. It reminded Daniel of how the world felt before a thunderstorm.

They had travelled some way along another alleyway, a shortcut completely hidden from the streets, when Silver stopped dead and clamped a hand on Daniel's shoulder. A little further up the path, a man in a ragged black coat blocked the way. In his hand he clutched a dagger with a long curved blade that looked as though it had drawn blood many times.

"Give me your money and valuables," he said.

"We don't have any money." Mr Silver's voice was low and calm, but there was an undercurrent there, something sharp and dangerous.

The mugger smiled.

"You wear a fine suit such as that, and expect me to believe you've got no cash? I may be a mugger, but I'm not a mug." He held out his free hand, beckoning for Silver to hand over his wallet.

"Put the blade away," said Silver. "I do not like knives."

The mugger snorted.

"Well, I'm sorry to inconvenience your lordship," he said. "But the idea behind my holding this blade is not to make you feel more comfortable, is it?" He took a step forward, raised the blade so that it pointed to Silver's face. "Last chance."

Mr Silver did not move. He did not even blink.

The mugger's gaze turned from Silver to his own hand, the one that held the knife.

"What … what's happening?" Beads of sweat were forming on his forehead, dripping from the end of his nose. He began to shake, to gasp and squirm. "What … are you … doing?" he said through clenched teeth.

It was then that Daniel noticed the knife trembling in the mugger's hand, glowing red hot, like embers of coal in the Emporium's fire.

"I can't let go!" screamed the mugger. He dropped to his knees. "Help me! Please!" He crumpled on the ground in agony.

Mr Silver watched for a while, his face impassive. Then he made the slightest of movements, and the mugger's grip on the glowing dagger was released. The man whimpered, nursing his hand.

Mr Silver dusted a speck from his sleeve. He stepped over the mugger, motioning for Daniel to follow.

"I warned you," he said without so much as a backward glance. "I do not like knives."

CHAPTER 12

FRICTION

Edinburgh, August 1885

The dagger spun through the darkened theatre in perfect circular motions, blade glinting in the stage lights.

Across the stage, Vindictus Sharpe's apprentice was suspended several feet in the air, fastened securely to a sparkling circular board. The audience gasped as the blade plunged deep into the board only a few inches from his left eye, though the young man himself did not so much as blink.

As the crowd applauded, Vindictus Sharpe, widely regarded as the world's finest magician, held up his hand for quiet. Blindfold tied tight over his eyes, he reached down to the table by his side, his fingers touching upon the handle of another dagger.

Silence.

Sharpe raised the dagger to his shoulder, sent it ripping through the air with a flick of the wrist.

Again the apprentice remained calm. His thunder-grey eyes watched the blade with great concentration as it flew towards him. This time, the dagger stabbed deep into the board above his head, so close that a few of his wild dark hairs were now half an inch shorter. The audience seemed to breathe as one. Some of them could not bear to look as Sharpe reached for the last remaining dagger, preparing to launch it with his weaker left hand.

Another flick of the wrist, and the dagger was a blur in the frozen silence.

Someone in the audience screamed as the apprentice caught the blade between his teeth.

For an agonising moment, nothing happened.

Then the apprentice tilted his head back and spat the dagger high into the air. As it soared upwards, the blade shattered into many pieces, each blossoming and shifting and blurring, until there were two dozen red admiral butterflies fluttering above the stage.

The audience roared. They stood in the aisles. They whistled and cheered.

Sharpe freed his assistant from his bindings. The

young man took a quick bow, and slipped through the stage curtain. He swept through the darkened area backstage, down a set of wooden steps, and into the relative calm of the dressing room he shared with Sharpe.

He sat in a wicker chair and removed his necktie, observing his reflection in the mirrored dresser. Even down here, in the bowels of the theatre, the roar of the crowd was still audible. He could picture Sharpe strutting around the stage like a gigantic peacock, soaking up the applause he craved so much.

A knock on the door.

"Who is it?"

"Birdie."

A smile flashed across the young man's face. He darted up from the chair, grabbing a bunch of drooping white roses from a glass vase on the dresser. He waved a hand over the flowers. Clouds of colour instantly flooded the petals, billowing like ink through water. In a moment, he was holding what might have been a freshly picked bunch of roses, save for the fact that they were in shades that did not exist, deep blues and silver-greys.

"Come in!"

When Birdie entered, wearing a flowing gown of black and gold, he rushed to her, planting a kiss on her hand, pushing the flowers into her arms.

"You've learned some manners," she said, her

wrinkled mouth curling upwards at the corners. "You must be after something."

He offered her a drink, which she gladly accepted, and they sat on a comfortable couch.

"It seems we are a hit." She indicated the general direction of the stage. "Edinburgh lapped it up, every moment of it."

The young man made no reply. He scratched the tip of his nose.

Birdie frowned. "What is on your mind, boy?"

"I'm not sure I should say. I must remember my place."

"You are having doubts about our project," Birdie said.

For a long moment, he did not answer. Then he took a deep breath. "Not doubts exactly. More like … I'm struggling to understand the point of what we're doing. Every night I stand on that stage and I watch the faces in the crowd, knowing that they believe our show to be nothing but trickery and misdirection. They think we're fakes."

Birdie contemplated this.

"And what would you like to do instead?" she said, her voice calm and warm. "Tell them magic is real?"

"Of course not. I just want … I don't know. Something … bigger. I want to change the way they see the world."

Birdie frowned at him, but she could not hide the twinkle in her eyes.

"And what exactly might this 'something bigger' be?"

The apprentice hesitated, and then reached into the silk-lined pocket, bringing out a black leather book, similar in size to a diary.

"I have ideas," he said, waving the book in the air. "Would you look at them for me, Birdie? I don't expect any promises, but perhaps if you like some of my concepts, you can talk to him. He'll listen to you—"

He stopped. Vindictus Sharpe stood in the doorway like a great bear, his blue eyes blazing. He waved his hand, and the black book broke free of the young man's grip, zipping across the room into his waiting palm.

The apprentice cringed as his mentor thumbed through several of the pages.

"You have spent a great deal of time on these ideas, haven't you?"

The apprentice felt a little hope rise in his chest. He nodded. "Yes, sir."

"And you believe you have the skill to pull these off successfully?"

Another nod.

Sharpe began to laugh. But it was not laughter of good humour, or affection. It was a laugh designed to hurt. "Then you are deluded," he said, and he tossed the book to the floor.

"Vindictus! Is that necessary?" said Birdie.

"I will not tolerate the arrogance of a teenager with ideas above his station!" spat Sharpe. He strode to the dressing table and poured himself a large drink, downing it in one. Then he opened his arms, motioning around the room. "You think that you are better than this?"

"No, sir," said the apprentice. "Of course not. I don't wish to seem ungrateful—"

"Then keep your mouth shut. Focus your energy on the skills I am trying to teach you – skills that are making you a wealthy young man, if I'm not mistaken."

"But—"

Sharpe threw his glass with such force that his apprentice barely had time to react. The young man shot up a hand at the last second, and the glass changed direction, bending around his head, shattering against the wall.

"Enough of this!" said Birdie. She did not raise her voice, but the severity of her tone was enough to capture even Sharpe's attention. He turned away and sat at the dresser, filling another glass.

Birdie placed a hand on the apprentice's shoulder.

"I think it best if you go ahead to the hotel and give Vindictus a little time to cool off. He was under great pressure this evening. Opening night in Edinburgh can crack even the hardest egg, yes?"

The young man managed a half-smile. "As you say, I shall see you here tomorrow. Good night."

He kissed Birdie on the cheek and exited without another glance at Sharpe. He was so flustered that he did not remember to pick up his book from the floor.

When she was sure the boy had gone, Birdie retrieved the book and sat on the comfortable couch, flipping through the pages.

"Don't chase him away," she said without looking up. "He is not like anyone else. You can take almost any urchin from the streets and teach him how to turn a rag into a pretty scarf. But talent like his is rare, as you have insisted on telling me over the years. His ideas are exceptional."

Sharpe glared at her in the mirror.

"He is not as talented as he believes. He needs a lot of work. He must be reminded of this now and again."

"How? By almost killing him with a glass to the head? I can see what's really going on, Vindictus. You are intimidated by the boy's abilities. You see him as a threat to your crown."

Sharpe did not respond, choosing instead to fill his glass for a third time.

Birdie stood up and leaned heavily on her cane as she limped to the door.

"Goodnight, Vindictus. I hope to find you in better spirits tomorrow. A word of warning: the boy is too talented to waste. If you cannot work with him, then I will find someone who can."

She left without saying another word, and was escorted through the plush red-carpeted corridors of the theatre into a waiting carriage. As the horses carried her off through the warm Edinburgh night, Birdie turned the book over in her old hands, reading and re-reading the inscription on the cover:

The Wonders of Lucien Silver

CHAPTER 13

THE GOLDEN RULE

Daniel followed Mr Silver back through the streets of Paris. He wasn't entirely sure what Silver had done to the mugger in the alley – only that it had not been anything good. The look in Silver's eyes told him not to ask. Not today.

When they reached the Nowhere Emporium, Daniel's spirits lifted the moment he saw Ellie. She sat with her feet on Mr Silver's desk, flipping through the browning pages of a newspaper that might have been a hundred years old. When she looked up, her eyes flicked from her father to Daniel and back, and her face hardened and flushed.

"Had a good time, have we?" she said.

"Not really, no," said Silver. He melted into his

chair and reached into the desk, fetching a bottle of whisky and a glass. He poured a small amount, and sipped.

Ellie ruffled his hair. "Papa…" she said, in a sickly sweet voice, "you know my birthday's coming up? I want to talk to you about it."

Mr Silver's eyes were shut. He was massaging his head.

"Can it wait?"

"But it's my birthday," said Ellie through gritted teeth.

Silver opened one eye.

"Your birthday?"

She folded her arms. "Didn't I just say that? It's next month, remember? I've had a few ideas about the ball this year."

Silver reached into his pocket and brought out his *Book of Wonders*, stowing it away in the desk. "Ellie, I've had a rotten morning. Can we please talk about this tomorrow?"

Ellie let her arms fall to her sides. "It's always tomorrow. Or the day after that. Or next week. It's always later. While you're out and about with your new best friend," she pointed to Daniel, "I'm stuck here every day. And you can't even find five minutes to talk about my birthday! You don't care about me. You never have." She stormed towards the curtain and disappeared.

A moment later, she poked her head back into the shop and added, "I hate you."

Then she was gone.

Silver scrambled up, knocking over an inkwell on his desk. He went after Ellie, leaving ripples spreading through the velvet curtain, and black ink seeping across his desk.

Daniel didn't know what to do. He was more certain than ever that Ellie must hate him. And he could understand why. He had been brought to the Emporium to do what Ellie couldn't: to learn about magic and Wonders and all the rest.

He grabbed an old newspaper and began soaking up the spilled ink from Silver's desk. As he worked, something caught his eye. One of the drawers in the desk was open a fraction. Daniel leaned to shut it, but a glint of light from within caused him to pause. Without knowing why, he opened the drawer. He felt a flutter in his chest.

Inside the drawer was Mr Silver's *Book of Wonders*.

In all the commotion with Ellie, Mr Silver hadn't locked the drawer.

Daniel stared at the book. Anticipation began to build inside him. Ever since he'd written his first Wonder, something had been playing on his mind. It seemed to him that anything was possible, that there were no limits to what the stroke of a pen could achieve inside these walls. And if that was the case, if anything was possible, then why couldn't he see his parents again?

Mr Silver's warning echoed in his mind: "*If, by some tiny chance, you ever come across the book when you are alone, I must ask that you do not write a single word in its pages without me.*"

Daniel tried to turn away, to close the drawer and forget about it, but he could not shake the notion that had gripped him. His heart ached to hold the book, to write in its pages, to open a door and see his parents' faces – faces that he could barely remember. He could almost feel their arms wrapping around him.

And anyway, hadn't he been creating Wonders of his own for days and days, all of them perfect? Surely it wouldn't hurt to add another?

A final glance at the curtain, and Daniel snatched the book from its place in the drawer. He rested it with great care on the desk, and turned to a blank page. He grabbed one of Mr Silver's fountain pens. He dipped the pen in what was left of the puddle of ink, and lowered the shining nib to the page, hardly daring to wish or hope.

The nib of the pen found the page, and he began to write.

Ten minutes later, Daniel was sweeping through the Emporium towards his new Wonder. He hurried up a narrow staircase, turned a sharp corner into a passage with a low ceiling.

For a moment, he forgot to breathe.

The new door was just up ahead. But everything was very wrong. Something inside, something huge and angry, was banging and pounding on the door, straining to get out. Guttural screams filled the air as the door juddered and shook.

And as terrible as all of this was, as confused and scared as it made Daniel, the worst thing of all was not the beast behind the door. No. The very worst thing was that Mr Silver stood by the new door, arms folded, thunder-grey eyes glaring down the corridor. In his hands, he held the *Book of Wonders*.

"What did you do?" he asked. His voice was calm and low, which unsettled Daniel more than if he had yelled.

The door rattled. A howl came from the creature beyond. In that moment Daniel wished to be anywhere else – even back on the streets of Glasgow, running from Spud and his gang.

"I … I wanted to see my parents," he said, amazed he could still speak. "Every day, they get a bit further away, a bit harder to remember. When I picture them, they're sort of fuzzy round the edges. So I wrote a room where they're still alive."

Silver's shoulders seemed to sag a little. He looked old and hunched. And then he straightened up and was himself again. Something battered the door with the force of a train. Daniel jumped back.

"Magic cannot bring back the dead, Daniel," said Silver, and he began to flip through the book, stopping when he found the page on which this Wonder had been written. Another scream, and the corridor trembled. "There are certain borders that should not be crossed. The line between the living and the dead is one of them; if we mess with that, we create cracks that allow terrors beyond imagination to escape, nightmares that have been trapped for eternities." He pointed to the door.

"Will it get out?" said Daniel.

"If it did, we would all be in trouble," said Silver. He ripped the page from the book, and at once the bricks around the doorway began to shift, closing in around the door, sliding and swivelling into place until the doorway was buried beneath, the wall blank and clean. Then Silver held out his hand, and the page caught fire. Daniel watched it curl and blacken, and soon nothing remained but floating whispers of cinder.

Silver wagged a finger at Daniel.

"If you had told me you wished to see your parents," he said, "I might have been able to create an image from your memories – an echo of what has passed. But they would not have been real. The dead are beyond the reach of magic. Do you understand?"

Daniel nodded.

"You have failed the second test," said Silver, stowing the book away.

"Test?" said Daniel. And then it came to him: Silver had left the drawer unlocked on purpose, giving Daniel access to the book. How could he have been so stupid, so easily tempted? He wished that he could go back and change things, that he had left the book in its drawer. Everything was ruined.

"Are you going to sack me?" he asked quietly.

Silence.

Silver stared at Daniel, seemed to be staring through him.

"What you did was dangerous," he said. "What if I hadn't been watching? What if a customer had come along and opened that door? Do you understand what you've done? Not only have you disobeyed me, you've used the book selfishly, and hurriedly."

Daniel felt small and ashamed. He felt like a thief.

"I'm so sorry," he said, and to his surprise there were tears in his eyes. Real tears. He took a breath, and fought them back. "If you want to drop me back in Glasgow, I understand. It's my own fault. I'm the one who ruined everything. But I promise you I've learned my lesson."

Silver let out a long, wheezing cough. He leaned against the wall until it stopped.

"I will give you one final chance," he said, and he

held up a finger to silence Daniel's thanks. "But you must be punished. You have a connection with the *Book of Wonders*. That much is obvious. I won't break that connection. But I will not permit you to write a single word in its pages until I feel you are ready. If you put even one foot out of place, you will be gone."

Daniel wanted to jump up and down. Instead, he pushed his relief and delight back down inside.

"Thanks, Mr Silver," he said. "I promise I won't let you down."

Silver raised an eyebrow, and the lines around his eyes seemed to deepen.

"You had better not."

CHAPTER 14

TRUCE

Since his run-in with the mugger in Paris, Mr Silver had not been the same. Aside from putting a stop to any lessons (which Daniel missed greatly), Silver treated him well enough. Still, there was no denying that something was not right. His limp was showing no signs of improvement, and his general health seemed to be worsening each day. He looked older somehow, tired and fragile, and at times he would simply sit staring into space while cups of tea grew cold and customers came and went. His production of new Wonders had slowed to a halt. Daniel was worried about him, and about the Emporium.

Silver moved the shop around a lot over the next few weeks, visiting Berlin in the 1930s, as Hitler was riding the crest of a dark wave; London during the coronation of Queen Victoria; and finally, the streets of Barcelona just months after the end of the Spanish Civil War. In each of these places and times, Silver would scour the backstreets for magical shops, searching for his elusive treasure. But he would always return empty-handed and angry.

One morning in Barcelona, Daniel set out to fetch coal for the fire. Upon his return to the shop, he began to tidy in preparation for twilight. He listened to the ticking of the clocks as he worked, humming tunes and tapping on the tables and books.

"You should be on stage with a voice like that."

Daniel, who had been polishing the eagle feet of Mr Silver's desk, sprang up, catching the edge of the table with a thud.

Ellie stood by the velvet curtain, arms folded. Daniel had not seen her since Paris. He knew that she didn't like him – and why should he like her? She seemed pig-headed and infuriating. But he found her fascinating.

"Where've you been?" he said.

Ellie shrugged. "Around."

"I've been watching out for you," said Daniel. "I've … well, I've been wanting to say something: sorry."

Ellie tilted her head a little. "Sorry?"

"Aye," said Daniel. "I mean … I can understand if you hate me. Some wee boy from Glasgow coming in here and getting a job. Working with your dad. But, Ellie, I don't really have a clue what I'm doing! I'm sorry I didn't know about you, about how you're stuck in here. I'm just…"

"Sorry?" said Ellie.

Daniel nodded.

"Daniel Holmes," she said, unfolding her arms, "however it might seem sometimes, I promise you that none of this, none of my storming off and throwing strops and getting angry, is really about you. Well, not much of it anyway."

"It's not?"

"Nope. Look. Papa and me, we have … well, we don't have a very smooth relationship. I love him to bits, really I do. But I get so angry with him sometimes. It always seems like I'm the least important thing on his list, even if I know that's not really true. And you … well you were just another distraction."

"I didn't mean to be," said Daniel. "I didn't ask to come here."

"I know," said Ellie. "I know. That's the point, I guess. Neither of us asked to come here. But here we are."

"Is it really true you can't leave?" said Daniel.

Ellie ran her fingers over the point of her chin. "Yes."

"And the customers can't see you?"

"Nope."

"Is it, like, a magic disease or something?"

Ellie laughed. "It's complicated."

"Well, I can see you," said Daniel. "You've got someone else to talk to. I mean. If you want."

Ellie stared at him, the corners of her mouth forming the tiniest smile. "You want to see something cool?"

Twilight came and went, and the Emporium opened its gates to the public.

"What are we doing?" whispered Daniel. They had followed a customer, a man in a flat cap, through the Emporium, keeping out of sight, watching him enter several Wonders. Along the way, they passed Caleb and Anja, who tagged along, quite delighted to be a part of whatever was going on.

"You'll see," said Ellie. They reached a quiet passageway where the customer in question entered another Wonder. "This'll do," said Ellie. To Daniel she said, "You. Stay." Then to Caleb and Anja, "You know what to do."

Daniel ducked behind a coat of armour just as the man reappeared. He watched Ellie walk towards him.

She's going to bang into him! Daniel thought.

But Ellie did not bump into him. She walked straight through him, like she was made of mist. The customer shivered, rubbed his hands together. He glanced around the dim corridor.

"Is … someone there?" he said in a quiet voice.

Nobody answered.

Ellie ran a little way down the corridor, to where another suit of armour was standing, and she began to push the armour along the ground towards the customer. When he heard the shrieking, scraping noise of the armour on the floor, the man jumped, and turned just in time to see the suit of armour emerging from the shadows. He screamed, twisted round, and ran right into Anja, who stood tall, every inch of her covered in undulating, glistening snakes. The man shrieked, and spun again, just as Caleb lit his torch and blew hard on the flame, making the tongues lick and curl into the shape of a monster. In his panic, the man ran into a wall and then went sprinting away, back towards the hall of stairways.

Ellie was laughing so hard she was bent double.

"Did you see his face?" said Caleb, tears of laughter streaming down his cheeks. He mimicked the poor customer. "That was one of the best in ages!"

The laughter was catching, and Daniel was soon slumped on the floor beside the other three.

"This is how you pass the time?" he said. "Isn't it a wee bit mean?"

"Oh, I don't do it often," she said. "But it usually works if I need cheering up." She wiped her eyes.

"Customers don't remember anything after they leave the shop, do they? So it's perfectly harmless to scare them half to death!" Her brain seemed to switch gears. "Hey, we're having a ball for my birthday soon. You'll be invited."

Daniel, who had never been invited to a party in his life, opened his mouth to accept, but Ellie was talking again...

"Papa throws the best balls for my birthday. I think it's his way of making up for the fact he's so completely obsessed with the Emporium for the rest of the year. All of the staff will be there." She nodded to Caleb and Anja. "Won't you?"

"Of course!" said Caleb. "Have we ever missed a ball?" He clapped his hands together. "Oh, I love mixing with people from the real world." He stopped short, remembering that Ellie would be nothing but a ghost to many of her own birthday guests.

"Don't worry," she said. "It's nice to have so many people there just for me. They can't see me, of course, but I enjoy watching them, listening to how they talk, hearing their stories from out there."

"Where has everyone gone today?" said Daniel. They had been walking back through the Emporium as they talked. There was no sign of customers or staff. The place had fallen silent. "It's too early for closing time."

"Something's up," said Ellie.

They said goodbye to Caleb and Anja and rushed

down staircase after staircase, seeing no one, until they were on the ground floor, through the red curtain to the shop front.

The CLOSED sign had been hung on the door. Mr Silver, limping and wheezing, was busying himself at the strange instrument on the wall. He was twisting dials as if his life depended on it, an expression of panic on his handsome face.

Ellie leaned close to Daniel and whispered, "He's lost his marbles. It's finally happened."

Daniel squinted at Mr Silver, who was now tossing handfuls of coal haphazardly at the fire.

"We're leaving?"

"Very perceptive of you."

"Why so sudden? What's happened?"

"I've decided I don't like Barcelona."

Daniel glanced at Ellie, who gave him her best 'I told you so' look.

The fire roared. The flames turned red.

"I'm supposed to be your assistant," he said. "If something's wrong, maybe I can help?"

Silver stopped. He turned and fixed Daniel with wild grey eyes.

"Nobody can help."

Daniel didn't get the chance to ask another question. The fire exploded in a cloud of soot. By the time the dust had settled, Mr Silver had disappeared through the curtain.

CHAPTER 15

BIZARRE'S BAZAAR

The Nowhere Emporium arrived in New York on 30th October 1929.

"It has a magic all of its own, this city," said Mr Silver, staring through the sepia tinted window from behind his desk. "The buildings — skyscrapers they call them — are growing taller by the day, it seems. It is as if they are racing to touch the sky. There is no place like it."

Daniel turned from the impressive view and watched Mr Silver, who was half hidden behind a pile of black envelopes, scribbling on small black cards. A silver magpie sat on each shoulder.

"What are those for?" asked Daniel, scrubbing a layer of soot from the mirrors and clocks.

"Invitations," said Silver. He did not elaborate.

"It's for my birthday ball," Ellie told him later. "It's tomorrow."

Daniel and Ellie had begun to meet most days before the Emporium opened to the public. Ellie, for all of her fierce bravado, was also caring and loyal, and Daniel had seen flashes of the person she hid behind her armour. It was also useful to be in Ellie's company; he was still banned from writing in the book, and Mr Silver seemed too distracted to teach him much. Ellie was the next best thing – a guide who knew every corner of the Emporium.

Daniel supposed that loneliness was binding them together. He was an orphan after all, and Ellie was motherless and always chasing the attention of her father. So here they were, two lonely children sharing in the biggest, most incredible secret there ever was.

A smile spread across Ellie's face. "When Papa's finished the invitations, you can help me send them out. It'll be fun!"

"Fine," said Daniel, unable to fathom why anyone would get so excited about posting some letters. His mind turned to Mr Silver. "Ellie, have you noticed anything strange about your dad recently?"

"He's always strange," said Ellie.

"I mean a different sort of strange. Not in a good way. He spends most of his time alone, either locked up in his apartments or out looking for some secret object. I think he might be ill. He's been limping and coughing and all sorts."

Ellie considered this for about four seconds.

"I'm sure he's fine," she said with a shrug.

Daniel left it at that, knowing Ellie was too excited about her birthday ball to think about anything else.

That evening, twilight came and went, but Mr Silver did not open the Emporium.

"Is something wrong?" asked Daniel. "Are we having a night off?"

Silver looked hollowed and worn. He did not answer, but slipped on his coat.

"Going out?" said Daniel.

Silver gave a nod. "Come if you like."

Eager to explore Manhattan, Daniel was across the room in a few bounds, pulling on his coat and gloves and scarf. Together they set off into the night.

As it turned out, sightseeing was not on the agenda; it soon became clear that Mr Silver was on the hunt again for his elusive treasure. He limped a couple of steps ahead of Daniel, barely speaking as they charged along streets carved like canyons through the enormous buildings.

Central Park. Among all the suffocating concrete and glass and fog, it seemed like the last green place on earth. Mr Silver pointed out the famous Plaza Hotel, an enormous building that looked like a grand castle. Eight blocks later, they swung into an alley where the steam from restaurant kitchens glowed in the light of the moon. They walked until they reached a plain brown door. At first glance it seemed to be the back entrance to a store or café or hotel. But then Daniel spotted something: two words carved into the doorframe above the door, the sort of thing that would only be noticed by those searching for it.

BIZARRE'S BAZAAR

Silver leaned in and opened the door.

The shop beyond was a dark and dingy cave, half-lit by the soft, flickering glow of hundreds of dribbling candles. The air was soup-thick.

Mr Silver had packed the Nowhere Emporium with many trinkets and objects picked up on his travels – "props", he called them – that would never be sold, but created the illusion of a regular store. You could spend hours looking and always spot something you'd never seen. But Bizarre's Bazaar must have contained a hundred times the amount of treasures. Coats of armour glistened. Swords and shields hung on great racks. There were jars of pickled animals, powders, lotions, potions, cages containing ravens and snakes and spiders the size of Daniel's fist.

At the far end of the store stood a counter, and behind the counter sat a middle-aged man with greasy, receding hair and a long, waxy face. His eyes seemed too large for his head, and one of them pointed inwards while the other fixed on his customers.

"You lookin' for somethin' in particular?" he said in a voice rough as dead tree bark.

"As a matter of fact," said Mr Silver... He leaned in and whispered something in the man's ear. At first the shopkeeper did not respond. He sat back in his chair and reached under his desk, and when he brought his hand back up it held a large onion. He raised the onion to his mouth and took a bite, skin and all, as if it were a juicy apple.

"You're in luck, friend," the shopkeeper said, onion juice dripping from his yellow teeth.

Silver took a sharp intake of breath. He closed his eyes for a moment. When he opened his eyes there was a spark in them that Daniel had never seen before.

"Show me."

The shopkeeper's yellowing eyes lingered on Silver's dusty old suit.

"You realise," he said, "that the item in question will not be cheap?"

"Show me!" roared Silver, and he brought his fist down on the counter with such force that Daniel actually jumped.

The shopkeeper nodded and cowered and turned away, disappearing down a set of stairs somewhere behind the desk. There was much banging and clattering from an unseen room, and after several minutes he reappeared, carrying a thin wooden box decorated with intricate carvings. Mr Silver took it in his hands, and turned his back to both Daniel and the shopkeeper.

A pause.

Daniel heard the box snap shut, and Silver spun around. His face was blank, but there was a light dancing somewhere deep in his eyes.

"I'll take it," he said, and he reached into his coat and pulled out a huge wad of hundred dollar bills, held together with a golden clip. He tossed the money onto the desk. It was more money than Daniel had ever seen, or imagined, and he watched the shopkeeper's eyes widen and his face become a mask of avarice and hunger. He dropped his raw onion to the floor and wiped the drool from the corner of his mouth, scooping up the money and cradling it in his hands like a baby.

"Do we have a deal or don't we?" Silver asked impatiently.

"Oh yes," said the shopkeeper, and he held out a long hand that was both the colour and texture of blue-veined cheese. "We have a deal all right. We have a deal."

CHAPTER 16

INVITATIONS

"So what was it?" asked Ellie, leading Daniel into a golden elevator in the Nowhere Hotel. "What did he buy?"

"I couldn't tell," said Daniel. "He rushed straight back to the Emporium and locked himself away." He shook his head. "Something's not right, Ellie. I mean, you should have seen the way he acted in that shop, all aggressive and … and desperate."

The elevator opened and they walked along a plush hotel hallway and knocked on the door to room 108.

"Yes, yes, coming, coming," said a voice from inside.

"Why do we need Caleb and Anja to help us with a few invitations?" asked Daniel.

Ellie smirked. "You'll see."

The door opened, and the doorway was completely filled by the huge body of Caleb the fire-breather. He smiled down at Ellie. "That time of year already, eh?" He stepped aside, allowing Anja the snake-charmer out of his room. She was holding a set of playing cards, and she waved them in front of Caleb's face as she passed.

"Seems I'm on a roll," she said. "Remind me, Caleb, what was the final score?"

Caleb muttered something under his breath, then shut the door with a bang and said, "Let's go before Anja's head becomes too big to fit through the lobby, hmmm?"

They made their way from the opulence of the Nowhere Hotel to the cold, sparkling emptiness of the Emporium's corridors. In the great hallway of staircases, they climbed up and up, flights of stairs moving and grumbling around them, until they arrived in what seemed to be a huge stockroom. On one side, the high walls were stacked with rack upon rack of glittering clothes in shades of orange and gold and black. On the other, a great variety of black iron birdcages sat on wooden shelves. All were empty. There was a table, where Mr Silver's magpies sat preening their glistening wings. Beside them was a high pile of black envelopes.

"Aren't these the invitations Mr Silver was writing yesterday?" Daniel asked.

"Yep."

"You want me to take them to the post office?"

Ellie gave a laugh. "No, that's fine," she said. "We'll send them the usual way."

"What's that?"

"You'll see. Take a seat at the desk and yell out the name written on the first envelope, will you?"

Daniel held the invitation in his hands, and he watched Ellie stroll over to the high racks of clothes, followed closely by Caleb and Anja and the magpies. There were ladders on rails attached to the racks, so that you could climb up and move freely along the rows.

"This one says Mr Radcliff Bone," he yelled.

Ellie gave a nod, and began to climb the ladder, moving back and forth along the rows of clothes with the magpies flapping around her head. "This will do," she said, reaching up for a glistening black suit studded with glowing orange stones. She held the suit out for the magpies, and the birds swooped down and snatched it from her hands, dropping it onto the counter in front of Daniel.

"What now?" he asked.

"Lay the clothes out on the table and put the invitation on top."

Daniel laid the suit out as best he could. He placed the envelope on top. No sooner had the paper touched the material than the suit began to move, arranging

123

itself one fold at a time into a tightly packed shape. When the final fold was complete, the suit was no longer just a suit. It was a bird. The material had arranged itself into the form of a huge raven, with wings of shining black silk and a beak studded with amber stones. Its eyes were two large orange buttons.

"Um … Ellie. Is the suit supposed to turn into a bird?"

"Of course!" Ellie's reply was casual, as though this was perfectly ordinary. "Grab it and put it in one of the cages before it tries to fly off!"

The crow was already spreading its huge wings. Daniel snuck towards it. It stared at him with button eyes. He made a leap towards the bird and wrapped his arms around it. Then he carried it, flapping and thrashing, to one of the cages stacked nearby. When the cage was locked, he wiped the sweat from his brow and gazed up at Ellie, who was clearly having a great time watching him struggle.

"Good job, Daniel," said Caleb, who was climbing a rack of his own. "Now back to work – we've only got another 150 to go!"

That night, as the clock ticked towards midnight, Daniel, Ellie, Caleb and Anja carried 151 cages to the front of shop. Caleb and Anja, of course, could not pass through the red curtain. Several times Daniel saw Caleb eagerly snatching a glimpse through the curtain towards the window to the real world. When all of the cages had been brought, Caleb and Anja headed off back towards the Nowhere Hotel.

"You want to play some more cards?" Anja said as they walked away.

"No. No way." Caleb waved his hands in front of him. "I have already been humiliated enough."

"Well … we could play something more suited to your small brain," said Anja. "Snap, perhaps?"

Daniel chuckled to himself as they disappeared from sight.

"Hey. A little help here?" Through the curtain to the shop, Ellie was arranging the cages. They didn't only contain birds; the costumes had also folded into shimmering black cats and huge golden rats, silken foxes and velvet bats, each fashioned from glistening materials in the colours of All Hallows' Eve.

Mr Silver was absent, as Daniel had come to expect, but Ellie assured him her father had given his word he would be attending the ball.

"We're cutting it close," said Daniel, noting that the many Emporium clocks pointed to five minutes to midnight. And then it struck him that the shop, usually alive with the whirring and ticking of clockwork, had become silent. Every clock had stopped.

Ellie carried the first cage to the Emporium

entrance and opened the door to the freezing New York night. She unlocked the cage. An orange velvet cockatiel with sparkling diamond eyes launched into the dark, its wings silent against the midnight air. Cage by cage, Daniel and Ellie released the animals. Each headed towards the address scrawled upon the invitation at its heart.

Every invitation arrived at its destination. From modest apartments to grand townhouses and hotels, they squeezed through letterboxes, or down chimneys, or through open windows. They snuck to the bedrooms of the invited guests and unfolded at the foot of their beds.

The invited guests did not know what had awakened them from their dreams, or even if they were really awake at all. They discovered mysterious envelopes that contained small black cards promising the chance of a lifetime – the opportunity to attend an enchanted ball.

And they found clothes. Ball gowns of deepest black velvet and burning orange silk; crystal tiaras decorated with flourishes of gold; diamond rings and golden necklaces; tuxedos and top hats and tails. Each item fitting perfectly, as if made to measure.

When they were dressed, the guests made their way through the streets, drawn towards the Emporium like sleepwalkers through enchanted dreams.

They approached the shop, and came together,

standing silently in neat rows, neither asleep nor awake.

None of them noticed when Vindictus Sharpe slipped from the shadows and joined the gathering crowd. He was not attired in Halloween shades like everyone else. He wore a finely tailored suit the colour of charcoal, and carried a silver-topped cane. His silver hair and moustache were neat, and his eyes were an unnatural, electric blue.

Strolling through the queue, Sharpe selected one of the guests, reaching over an elderly man's shoulder, plucking the invite from his hands. Then he whispered something in the old man's ear, and at once the old man turned and began to walk dreamily away from the Emporium, heading for home.

When every guest was present, the frozen clocks kicked back to life, filling the night with their ticking. The Emporium's delicate golden gate turned to dust and scattered in the crisp New York breeze. The queue began to filter in.

Sharpe moved up the line in silence.

Guests were disappearing behind a heavy red velvet curtain, awakening as they crossed the threshold. There were two doormen on the other side, collecting tickets and directing wonderstruck guests towards the ballroom.

Sharpe handed over his stolen ticket and walked past them.

He was in.

CHAPTER 17

GHOSTS

"Ellie! This is your fault."

Daniel stormed down a passageway of shimmering black brick, trailing Ellie behind.

"Sorry," she said, trying not to laugh. "You look great. Really."

"This," said Daniel, grabbing a handful of the black lace ruffles spilling from his orange suit, "does not look great! How could it possibly look great?" He turned and strode off with as much dignity as he could.

"How many times do you want me to apologise?" asked Ellie, catching him up. "Papa asked me what I thought you might like to wear. I couldn't resist. Don't tell me you wouldn't have done the same to me, because I know you would!"

"I'll get you back for this."

They reached a grand set of arched black doors. A single word had been painted on its nameplate in flowery letters:

Daniel pulled on the golden door handles, and the doors swung open.

A huge, circular Wonder opened up before him, with a marble floor and a high domed ceiling of deepest black, finished with scattered golden stars. The wall of the ballroom was made entirely of glass, circular and continuous, looking out towards the illusion of a clear night sky and an impossibly large full moon.

The floor was crowded with guests in orange, black and gold. Many had been cornered by members of the Emporium staff, who were excited by the rare opportunity to speak freely with those from beyond the shop's walls. Ghostly waiters walked among the guests. They carried golden trays neatly stacked with goblets of orange liquid, piles of chocolate bats and liquorice spiders, apples coated in rich caramel and chocolate, all filling the room with delicious sweet scents.

A hush began to fall over the crowd. Heads turned

towards a raised circular platform in the centre of the floor, where a ghostly brass band had assembled.

And then the band began to play.

Waves of music swept the ballroom, enveloping guests and staff alike, carrying them off into waltzes and spins and toe-tapping, high-kicking barn dances.

Daniel could not resist the urge to dance. He felt a hand on his arm, found himself on the floor with Anja, the snake-charmer. They danced until Daniel could dance no more, and he went to the edge of the room to catch his breath. Ellie showed no signs of stopping; she hadn't left the dance floor all evening, and it seemed to Daniel that this was the happiest he'd seen her look.

A waiter passed by, offering him a goblet.

"What is it?" he asked, trying not to be too distracted by the fact he could see through the waiter.

"Pumpkin mead."

Daniel took a goblet and sipped the liquid. It warmed his insides, like drinking the memory of an autumn night sat by the bonfire. He had drained the last drop from the glass when he turned and clipped the arm of an extremely tall man in a charcoal suit, dropping his goblet with a clatter.

"I'm sorry," said Daniel, but when he straightened up, the man was already gone.

Mr Silver walked the far side of the ballroom, sips of pumpkin mead warming him as he watched his daughter watching everyone else. He cut through circles of chattering guests, dodging waltzing couples, catching snippets of stolen conversation.

He smiled as he passed Caleb, who had cornered several guests from the outside world: "Tell me: is it true that the moon out there is made from cheese? And if so, what sort of cheese? Nothing too crumbly or runny, I'll bet..."

Silver stopped and finished his mead, glancing up at the chandelier high above.

Something in the corner of his eye bothered him.

He turned his head.

Everything – the music and the chatter, the graceful movement of the dancing guests, the waiters and the gleaming chandelier – seemed to stop.

Mr Silver's grey eyes fixed upon the blue eyes of the man striding through the crowd towards him. He recognised him at once.

As Vindictus Sharpe approached, he removed his bowler hat, stopping so close to Silver that their chests almost touched. The air crackled and sparked around them.

Mr Silver's face was as colourless as one of his ghostly waiters. His mouth was shut tight, his expression frozen, unreadable.

"You are a difficult man to find, Lucien," said Sharpe.

"I do my best," Mr Silver whispered.

Sharpe's mouth curled into something that might have been a smile, and might have been a sneer. He leaned in slowly, deliberately, and whispered something in Mr Silver's ear. Then he straightened up once more. He waited.

At first, Mr Silver did nothing but look at the floor. When he raised his head at last, his face was heavy with sadness.

He managed a slow nod.

Sharpe offered a handshake.

When their hands touched, lights around the hall began to flicker. A few bulbs blew out, spitting shards of glass among the feet of the guests, who gasped and shrieked and laughed, believing it to be part of the entertainment.

A flash of white teeth from Sharpe, and he turned and began to walk away through the crowd.

Mr Silver watched him as he left the ballroom, standing frozen among the sea of sparkling dancers.

CHAPTER 18

A PARTING OF WAYS

Edinburgh, May 1890

Raindrops the size of marbles pelted the fine oak coffin as it was lowered into the soil on an unseasonably cold Edinburgh spring day.

News of Birdie's passing had taken flight, crossing oceans and continents, and many of the entertainers with whom she had worked over the years had come to pay their respects, shivering together beneath a canopy of black umbrellas.

Lucien Silver stood near the mouth of the grave and listened as the minister delivered Birdie's eulogy. Vindictus Sharpe stood at Lucien's side, tall and dark and silent as a shadow. Neither acknowledged the presence of the other.

When the funeral was over, mourners began to filter away towards the shelter of waiting carriages. Lucien stayed by the graveside while Sharpe shook hands and exchanged brief words with a number of guests. When the last of the mourners was gone, he walked back up the hill.

They stood in silence for a time.

Sharpe turned his head, though not enough to make eye contact.

"Your services are no longer required," he said, flexing the fingers of a gloved hand. "This ... experiment has run its course. Teaching is not for me. I imagine this does not come as a shock to you?"

Lucien said nothing.

"You will be sent your portion of last night's takings, of course."

"I don't want it," Lucien said. "Last night's performance was for Birdie."

Sharpe gave a single nod. "Very well."

He turned and began the walk back down the hill.

Lucien gazed after him. "I can't help that I'm better than you," he said. "I only ever did what you asked, and I was good at my job. You turned it into a competition, not me."

He had uttered the words in barely more than a whisper. But in the silence of a graveyard, even soft-spoken words can become immensely powerful things.

Sharpe stopped. He did not turn around.

"You are not better than me," he said. There was an edge to his voice, dark and dangerous. "You will never be better than me. I rescued you from the gutter, and that is where I expect you to return now that you don't have my coat-tails to ride upon, or a foolish old woman like Birdie to protect you."

Lucien glared. "Must be strange for you, being in a graveyard, hmm? Considering you don't ever intend to die. I've always been too afraid to ask why you never get any older. But I think I might be piecing together the answer. You steal time from other people, don't you? You make their lives shorter so that you can extend your own. How can you live with yourself?"

A long silence.

At last, his back still turned, Sharpe said, "Goodbye, Mr Silver. Good luck."

Lucien watched his former employer wind down the path towards the comfort of his carriage. When the slick black horses had pulled Sharpe through the iron gates, it occurred to Lucien that a very long and interesting chapter of his life had come to an end.

He turned his attention once more to the fresh grave at his feet.

Reaching into his coat, he produced a single long-stemmed red rose. With the wave of a hand, the stem of the rose became black as coal, and the petals were coated in shining gold.

Lucien placed the black-gold rose on the headstone. "Goodbye, Birdie."

Rain washed the tears from his face as he trudged down the hill towards the gates and the world beyond. And the world was a big, big place. Lucien did not know where to go, or what to do next. His fingers touched the book in his coat pocket, its pages full of dreams, imaginings and possibilities, and somehow he did not feel quite so lost.

Without knowing why, he began to smile.

Then, with a final glance to the top of the hill, Lucien Silver walked through the cemetery gates and away.

CHAPTER 19

MISSING

Mr Silver vanished the day after Ellie's birthday ball. It was a Sunday, and the sky was heavy with black clouds and thunder.

"Papa has never missed opening time before." Ellie stood at the window, tapping her foot on the floor. "Something's wrong."

Daniel had to agree. In the few months he had been a part of Mr Silver's world, he'd never once seen his boss open the shop so much as a second late.

"I wonder if he…" Daniel's voice trailed away. Something lay on the floor under Mr Silver's desk. He picked it up and fanned through its many pages.

The *Book of Wonders*.

"Ellie, have you ever known your papa to leave this lying around?"

Ellie edged towards him. She reached out trembling fingers and touched the book.

"It looks like it's been ... it's been burned or something."

She was right. The ends of some of the pages were blackened, and Daniel found a cluster of shrivelled pages where Wonders had been scorched away. As they examined the book, a loose scrap of paper fell out. Ellie grabbed it.

"It's part of a note! From Papa!"

"What?" said Daniel. "What's it say? Let me see." He craned over her shoulder, and read:

Dearest Ellie (and Daniel Holmes),

I am sorry that I could not be there to give you this message in person. But time is against us. What you are about to read is frightening, but please, don't panic.

For reasons I do not have time to explain, the Emporium is in danger. Worse than that: it is becoming dangerous.

I have a plan. If you follow it to the letter you should be fine. You'll be safe in the shop front. Stay there whenever possible. And when the time comes, you must

The message ended abruptly.

"That's it?" said Daniel. "That can't be it!" He picked up the paper, stared at the ragged edge where the rest of the message had obviously been burned away. "Brilliant. Whatever burned the book destroyed the note as well, and your dad's plan."

Ellie was staring at the message, shaking her head.

"What's happened? What does he mean? That stuff about the Emporium being dangerous ... Where is he, Daniel?"

Daniel pointed to the coat stand. "Look. His coat is still hanging up. I don't think he's gone outside. Maybe we should just wait here like he says. I've ignored his orders before and it didn't end well."

Ellie shook her head.

"He only wanted us to stay here so we could follow his plan – and we don't know what that is, do we? We have to find him and tell him we're in the dark. He's probably relying on us, Daniel."

Mr Silver's apartments were the logical place to begin the search. They found the door open a fraction, and a labyrinth of grand chambers lay in wait, each made entirely from books.

As he searched, Daniel was distracted time and again by the strange and wonderful surroundings in which Mr Silver chose to live. He found Ellie in a garden of books, under a huge tree blossoming with intricately folded pages.

"He's not here," she said, and she kicked the trunk of the tree, shaking pages to the paper floor.

"Maybe we should go back to the shop?" said Daniel.

"But his note made it sound like he won't be back any time soon, didn't it?" Ellie said. "He's so infuriating sometimes, with his secrets! Why didn't he just tell us what's going on?"

"So we just keep looking, without a plan?" said Daniel. "How many rooms in the Emporium? A thousand? How are we supposed to check them all?" A thought flared to life in his mind. "Search parties!"

The lobby of the Nowhere Hotel was packed with impatient performers and vendors, eager to start work. This was the way of things: every day the staff would gather dressed to the nines in black and gold, checking pocket watches and timepieces until the glorious moment when twilight cloaked the world outside and the doors of the Emporium opened.

"'Scuse me. Sorry." Daniel pushed and squirmed through the pack, looking for Caleb and Anja. "Ouch! Watch it! Hey, there they are! Ellie, I found them!"

The fire-breather and snake-charmer were standing together, as they always seemed to be. Caleb stood a full head taller than everyone apart from Anja, and was holding court amid a group of vendors.

"So, out there in the real world, not only is the moon four hundred times smaller than the sun, it is four hundred times closer. So they appear the same size in the sky. And when they meet, the moon covers the sun completely! Day turns to night! And not a bit of magic is used! Now that is a wonder!"

Anja, who looked like she might fall asleep at any minute, caught sight of Daniel.

"Daniel! Ellie!"

Caleb broke off from his story. "What brings you two around here? And what's all this about?" he asked, pointing to the crowd. "We're late opening up. Never been late before."

"Papa's missing," said Ellie. "We found his *Book of Wonders* in the shop, all burned and bashed. And this note!" She handed the note to Caleb, whose face became grave.

"Missing?" he asked. "At opening time?" He exchanged glances with Anja. "That isn't right. No, no, no. Won't do at all."

"Will you ask the rest of the staff to search with us?" said Daniel. "It'd give us a better chance of finding him."

Caleb scratched the stubble on his square chin.

"I don't know," he said gravely. "What if he turns up? What if he suddenly opens the doors and none of us are anywhere to be seen because we're off searching the Emporium?"

"Read the note," said Daniel. "Doesn't sound like he'll be opening the Emporium, does it? He says it's dangerous. We need to find him, Caleb. We've got to know what's going on and what his plan is."

"If the Emporium's in danger, it means we're all in danger too," added Ellie. "I don't think Papa would abandon us. I think he's in here somewhere. We're worried about him, Caleb."

Anja said, "It does seem to be an emergency, Caleb. What if he's ill, or has fallen and banged his head? Or what if one of his Wonders is misbehaving?" She turned to Daniel. "It happens very rarely. Doors are left open. Things escape. Last time it was flying pencils. Very sharp."

Caleb gave a thoughtful nod. "That was an interesting day." He shook his big head. "But I'm sorry; we can't help. Rules are rules. We were created for one purpose: we must be ready always to take our posts."

Ellie looked crestfallen, but Daniel was getting an idea.

"I could make it worth your while," he said. "I could smuggle you something in from the outside world, eh? Come on. There must be something you want?"

Caleb peered down at him.

"Are you offering me a bribe, Daniel Holmes?"

"A bribe?" said Daniel, his eyes wide. "Not me. Just a gift. A way of saying thanks."

Caleb mulled this over. He scratched his big chin. "Very well. I want a kitten. A fluffy one." He shook Daniel's hand, then turned to the rest of the lobby. "Attention! We have a job to do!"

Word spread quickly through the lobby: Mr Silver was missing. Everyone was chattering and gossiping, agreeing that the loss of their leader was the worst disaster that could possibly happen.

"What'll we do without him?"

"We're lost!"

"This place won't last a week!"

And so the search was on.

There were many members of staff, many pairs of eyes and ears. They scoured the Emporium's catacomb of passages and doorways. They searched through vaults and tunnels in a basement that seemed to be mined into the earth. They climbed the very highest staircases, where the air was thin and cold and filled with crystal flakes of ice. They even rediscovered a long lost section of the Emporium, buried under a rainforest that had spilled from an open door.

But there was no trace of Mr Silver.

To add to the worry, many search parties returned

with news of strange cracks appearing on the Emporium walls, white lines crawling over black bricks like jagged spider trails. In some places it was worse than others. There was even a rumour that one of the corridors had collapsed.

"It is as if he has vanished," said Caleb, after yet another search party had reported no success. He clicked his fingers. "Gone. Poof. Like that. Are you very sure he hasn't left the shop?"

"He wouldn't leave the Emporium without the book," said Ellie. "It's practically part of him."

"Then I am sorry to say I'm stumped."

Daniel's mind was ticking. It just didn't add up. Why would Silver vanish? If the Emporium was in trouble, as his note suggested and the cracks in the walls confirmed, then Mr Silver would be the last to leave; Daniel knew that. And why had he dumped the book?

"Wait a minute," he said. "When we got to New York, Mr Silver finally found his 'treasure' – whatever he'd been searching for. And now, a few days later, he's gone. That can't be a coincidence, can it?"

"But what was the treasure?" said Ellie. "Was it something dangerous? And why would he disappear with it?"

Daniel shook his head.

"There's only one way to find out. I guess I'm heading back to Bizarre's Bazaar."

CHAPTER 20

BLOOD AND SNOW

"Are you sure about this?"

Ellie's nose was pressed against the glass of the Emporium's front window. She peered out into the wintry Manhattan darkness. Snow had begun to fall. It was now well after midnight, and Mr Silver had been gone an entire day.

"I'm sure," said Daniel, pulling on his coat and gloves and scarf.

"I wish I could go with you." To Daniel's great surprise, Ellie grabbed him and hugged him tight. "Be careful."

"I will. I'd better go."

The New York streets were eerily silent that night, every sound smothered by the thick layer of snow coating the city. Mostly, people had chosen not to brave the bitter cold and the ice-coated sidewalks.

Central Park seemed even bigger now that Daniel was alone, and the darkness brought with it the sort of characters who wished to go about their business unnoticed. He tucked his chin to his chest and hurried on, trying hard not to look at anyone. When he walked under a small footbridge, he imagined that someone was following, and began to run. He did not stop until he was past the Plaza. Eight blocks later, he spun into the alley and arrived at Bizarre's Bazaar.

There was only one other customer inside – a man in a long brown coat browsing row upon row of bottles.

Daniel approached the counter.

"Excuse me."

The shopkeeper, the one with skin like blue-veined cheese, had been examining a golden locket with a magnifying glass. At the sound of Daniel's voice, he looked up, one milky eye magnified through the lens.

"No refunds," he said, and he turned his attention back to the locket on the counter.

"What?"

"I never forget a face," said the shopkeeper. "Especially a face connected with so much cash. You were in here a few nights back with the rich man. Well, you can tell him from me: sending a kid isn't going to soften me any, oh no! I don't do refunds."

Daniel shook his head. "That's not why I'm here. I wanted to ask you about what you sold us the other night."

The shopkeeper looked up and smiled, showing Daniel a crooked row of rotten yellow teeth. "Ah. A very fine item."

"Was it?"

The shopkeeper leaned over the counter on folded arms. "Very fine. Let's just say it's not every day you come into possession of a vial of unicorn blood."

A crash from nearby; the second customer had dropped a metal box to the floor and was on his hands and knees scooping up the powder that had spilled.

"Hey!" yelled the shopkeeper. "Careful with the merchandise! You break it, you buy it!"

"Unicorn blood?" said Daniel. "Are you pulling my leg?"

"I'm not pulling anything."

"So you're telling me there are really unicorns out there?" Daniel had come to accept that the world was a far stranger place than he had ever imagined. Even so, a unicorn seemed a little far-fetched.

"Kid, if you know where to look, everything's out there."

"Why would someone want unicorn blood?"

The shopkeeper smiled. "Unicorn blood," he said, "is sometimes called Liquid Life. Just a few drops will cure you of your ills and boost your strength. It's very rare.

And very expensive, which is the quality I like best."

And there it was: what Daniel had hoped was not true. Silver was ill. There was no other explanation. And the treasure was a cure.

When he left the Bazaar, the cold of the night had sharpened, and the snow was falling harder. He pulled his coat and scarf tight, leaned into the wind as he walked.

In Central Park, trees sagged under the weight of the snow. Daniel's feet crunched through the sparkling white canvas, leaving footprints. When he reached the darkest part of the path, where it wound under the little footbridge, he was struck again by the strong sense that someone was following.

He cast a quick glance back the way he'd come.

He was not alone.

Through the falling snow, he saw a figure in a long brown coat, and recognised it as the customer he'd seen in the Bazaar. The figure slowed as Daniel turned, as though trying not to look suspicious. And then something happened – something that turned Daniel's spine to ice. Two glowing dots appeared on the figure's face, burning orange like cigarette ends.

They were eyes.

Daniel could see the entrance to the park, two hundred metres away.

He began to run.

Cold air burned his lungs as his feet pounded the

snow. The gate drew nearer with every step, but the man was catching up. Daniel's blood froze as a hand grabbed at his coat. He squirmed and yelped, managing to slip out of his coat, landing a wild blow to the man's ear. He broke free and tore through the gate to the streets. The Emporium was only a block away.

Daniel skidded between two parked cars, leapt onto the sidewalk. He ran and ran and ran, not looking back, imagining cold hands wrapping around his neck. Warm light poured from the shop window just a street away, and he thought he saw someone standing at the door, someone very tall…

Daniel's feet hit a frozen puddle. He landed hard on the ice, his knee taking the brunt of the impact. He looked up into a skeletal face, skin hanging loose, eyes glowing amber. The man chasing him was suddenly in front of him.

"Where's the unicorn blood?" said the old man. The voice was a rasping whisper.

"What? I don't have it! I swear!"

A hand crashed across Daniel's face. He tasted his own blood.

"I'm not messing around, kid. Tell me where the unicorn blood is—"

The man stopped mid-thought, gazed up at something. For half a heartbeat he was still, like a startled deer. Then his burning eyes grew wide and he turned and began to run. Something else brushed past Daniel, a blur of grey that was gone in an instant.

He gathered himself. He could feel hot blood seeping from his knee. The short walk across the street to the Emporium seemed to take forever.

"So who saved you?" said Ellie, back in the warmth of the shop. She was dabbing Daniel's knee with whisky from Silver's desk. It burned and stung.

"I don't know," he said through gritted teeth. "For a second I thought it was Mr Silver."

"I'd have seen him if it was," she said. She placed the whisky back on the desk. "There. Done. So you really think Papa is ill?"

"It makes sense," said Daniel, rolling his trouser leg back down. "The way he's been acting, how old he looks all of a sudden. He can't have bought the unicorn blood for anything else, can he? The shopkeeper said the stuff's famous for curing diseases."

Ellie took a long breath. "Why hasn't he told me?"

"He probably doesn't want you to worry."

"Daniel … what if the cure didn't work? What if we can't find Papa because he's gone somewhere far off in the shop to … to die? The plan he tried to leave us … it might have been instructions for what to do after he's gone."

The bell at the door sang out, and a deep voice said,

"Hello? Anybody here?"

"We didn't lock the door!" said Ellie. She wandered around towards the front door, where a tall, broad-shouldered man stood, silver hair and moustache glinting in the firelight. He wore an expensive-looking charcoal suit and carried a silver-handled cane. Electric blue eyes darted around the room, but he did not see Ellie; she was as much a ghost to him as to any other outsider who came into the Emporium.

The tall man spotted Daniel at the back of the shop, and moved towards him, passing straight through Ellie like she was made of nothing but light and shadow. He stopped in front of Daniel, staring down at him.

"Are you looking for something in particular?" Daniel asked.

"Not something," said the man. "Someone. I'm here to see Lucien Silver."

Ellie held up her hands, indicating she didn't know the stranger. "Nobody's ever come looking for Papa before."

"He's, um ... Mr Silver isn't available."

The tall man reached into his coat and produced a grey leather wallet. From the wallet he took a piece of paper and unfolded it. He handed the paper to Daniel. It was a clipping from a newspaper, some sort of review about a magic show. The date on the paper was 1884. There was a picture of two men. One of them was the man who stood before Daniel now, and he had not aged at all since the photograph was taken. The other man staring out from the picture was a teenage Mr Silver. There was no doubting it. Beneath the photograph, a caption read:

The incredible magic act of Vindictus Sharpe (right) and Lucien Silver is the talk of the theatrical scene.

Ellie scanned the clipping over Daniel's shoulder. "He knows Papa," she said.

"As you've probably gathered from the photograph, my name is Vindictus Sharpe," said the tall man. "I was – and remain – a friend of Lucien's." He took back the photograph and indicated the young Mr Silver. "In fact, I was his teacher."

"Somebody taught Mr Silver?" said Daniel.

Sharpe nodded. "I will come straight to the point. I am worried about Lucien. I attended his charming Halloween ball, and I was shocked to see how weak he has become. And now tonight, when I return to check on him, I find a child running the shop – the very same child I have just rescued from a mugger on the sidewalk."

"That was you?" said Daniel.

Sharpe waved the question away. "If you wish to repay me, tell me what is going on around here. Where is Lucien Silver?"

Daniel glanced to Ellie.

"I don't like him," she said. She sniffed the air around Sharpe. "He smells funny. And if he's such great chums with Papa, how come I've never heard of him?"

Ellie had been brought up by Mr Silver to protect the Emporium, to trust no one from the outside world. Daniel knew this. But these were desperate times. Silver was missing, and the Emporium was beginning to decay. Vindictus Sharpe had saved Daniel's life, and he seemed genuinely worried about Mr Silver. Surely Daniel owed him a chance?

"We don't know where Mr Silver is," he said. "He's missing — but we think he's somewhere in the Emporium. And we think he's ill. He bought unicorn blood. That's why I was mugged. The mugger heard me asking the shopkeeper about the blood and fancied some for himself, I guess."

Sharpe sat on the edge of a table piled high with golden coins. "This is most worrying," he said. "Why are you so sure Lucien is still inside the shop? Is there anything you're not telling me?"

Daniel was torn. His hand moved to the pocket of his jacket, to the *Book of Wonders*.

"Don't do it," said Ellie.

But it was too late. Sharpe's eyes were already on Daniel's hand.

"What have you got there?"

Daniel could do nothing but bring out the book.

"Mr Silver doesn't leave the shop without this," he said. "Not ever. We … I mean, *I* found it."

When he saw the cracked black cover, Sharpe made a tiny movement with his hand, as if he were about to reach out. His eyes did not leave the book as he said, "This is worse than I thought. I know Lucien, and I know all about that book. If he has left it behind, then he must be in real trouble."

Daniel watched Sharpe, who was watching the book. He slipped the book back into his pocket.

Sharpe flashed a smile. "You have written in the book. I can tell by the way you hold it."

Daniel looked to Ellie, who was staring back at him, her mouth open.

"Is it true?" she said. "Has Papa let you write in it?"

Daniel hung his head. He knew he'd technically done nothing wrong by writing in the book, but somehow he felt guilty for being able to do what Ellie couldn't, as if he was stealing a piece of her papa away from her.

"Yes," he said, both to Ellie and Sharpe.

Ellie nodded, but there was a faraway look in her eyes, and Daniel wished he'd been honest with her from the start.

Sharpe stood up, scattering a pile of golden coins across the table. "Then you understand what is at stake if Lucien is not found? It will be the end of all of this." He motioned around the room, and then pointed to the curtain with his cane. "The end of all that lies beyond."

Daniel had not wanted to think about this, although part of him knew the answer. The Emporium, and the people within its walls, couldn't survive without Mr Silver.

"Will you help?" he heard himself asking, though his voice seemed to come from somewhere far off. Panic was clouding his thoughts. He didn't wish to be ripped from a life of magic and friendship, from a place that felt like home.

Sharpe nodded. "Certainly I will. I hate to see an old friend in trouble. Lucien would do the same for me." He clapped his hands together and strode to the red velvet curtain. "I shall begin immediately. Rest up, Daniel Holmes – and join me whenever you wish."

And with that he was gone.

"I hope you know what you're doing," said Ellie. "Once you invite someone in, it can be very hard to get rid of them. I told you: Papa has never let anyone see behind the scenes before. Except you. There's a reason for that."

"He saved my life!" said Daniel. "And he's worried about Mr Silver."

"He's weird!" said Ellie. "I don't want anything to do with him." She pointed a finger in Daniel's face. "Sharpe's your responsibility. I'm going to help Caleb with the search for Papa."

"I'll come too," said Daniel.

"Oh, I don't think so," said Ellie. "You'll be far too busy keeping an eye on your new pal, won't you? A very close eye."

There was already a nagging doubt in Daniel's mind. Had he done the right thing, inviting a stranger into the shop? Surely someone who risked their own life to save his couldn't be bad?

"Ellie," he said, "about me writing in the book. I was going to tell you. I swear I was. I just—"

But Ellie was already gone.

CHAPTER 21

FEAR

Daniel had been walking with Sharpe for over an hour. They were searching one of the Wonders – an Egyptian pyramid filled with golden corridors – from top to bottom, because Sharpe thought Silver's magical trace was stronger there.

"You carry that book around like it's a great weight," Sharpe said, tapping the *Book of Wonders* with his cane through Daniel's jacket.

"Well, it sort of is," said Daniel. "All that power."

"Power is a good thing," said Sharpe.

"Aye, and dangerous too," said Daniel. "When I first came here, Mr Silver trusted me to write in the book. I was actually quite good at it. And then one day I wrote something without asking him. I thought

I knew what I was doing when really I didn't have a clue, and I nearly did some serious damage. Now Mr Silver wants me to wait until I'm ready for the responsibility."

Sharpe shook his head.

"Making mistakes is how we learn," he said. "I'll bet you are more ready than you think."

Sharpe spun left and stopped, sniffing at the air. He narrowed his eyes and touched a hieroglyph on the wall, causing part of the wall to open up, revealing a secret room. In the centre of the room sat a stone sarcophagus.

The dry air caught in Daniel's throat.

"You don't think … He's not in there, is he?"

Sharpe said nothing. He approached the tomb, which was shaped roughly like a man. He gripped the lid with his big hands, and pushed. Stone grated upon stone as the lid began to move, until there was a gap large enough to look through.

Daniel leaned over, praying Silver was not inside.

A fluttering explosion sent him tumbling back. A dark cloud of screeching bats erupted from the sarcophagus. They were in his hair, on his face, crawling on his skin. Sharpe grabbed Daniel and dragged him out into the main passage, slamming his hand on the hieroglyph. The doorway closed, locking the bats in their tomb.

"Definitely not in there," said Sharpe.

They left the pyramid, and began walking the

Emporium passageways. The cracks in the walls were becoming more pronounced, and fissures had appeared on some of the floors.

"Tell me, Daniel Holmes," said Sharpe after a while. "What are you scared of?"

The question came from nowhere, and it caught Daniel off guard. He thought for a moment, and then said, "Um, I ... I don't know."

Sharpe grinned. The stairs were getting steeper. Daniel struggled to keep pace. "You are frightened of something. I can smell it in the air around you. There is no shame in it, Daniel. But I will tell you this: whatever it is, whatever frightens you, it must be overcome. To be a truly great magician, you must be fearless. Lucien is the perfect example of a missed opportunity. I know him better than anyone. I've seen how his fears have bound him like chains, and I wonder what he might have achieved had he not spent his life running away."

"Running from what?" said Daniel.

Sharpe waved a hand in the air as though he was swatting away a fly. "That doesn't matter. What does matter is that he has wasted his life wrapped in this cocoon of sparkling black brick, cut off from the world rather than changing it. If you let your fears take root, boy, they'll grow and multiply. Fear is weakness."

"I don't think he's wasted his life."

"You are too young to know better," Sharpe said, turning the tail of the sentence into a laugh.

"Haven't you ever been scared?" said Daniel, and as the question left his lips, rain began to spit in the passageway. Sharpe stared down at him as they walked, and the droplets of rain began to bend around them, leaving them dry.

He did not answer the question.

They walked on in silence, and the subject of fear floated around in Daniel's mind, bubbling to the surface again and again until at last he felt he had to let it out.

"When I was a little boy, too little to properly remember, my dad died at sea. He was a fisherman. His boat went down in a storm with him inside it. Nobody could help him. He must've watched the water rise until there was nothing for him to do but breathe it in. Can you imagine what that must have been like?"

Sharpe did not look round. "That is not a pleasant way to die – if such a thing exists."

"I dream about it every night … I see him dying over and over. And I'm scared that it will happen to me."

Sharpe showed a spark of interest. "You are scared of drowning?"

"No. Not drowning. It's just that … well, I can't imagine how frightened he must have been, knowing the end was coming, knowing he only had a few breaths left. And in the end, in his final seconds, when he should have been with the people he loved, he had nobody. He died in the dark with nobody's hand to hold. I don't want to be alone—"

The world began to shake. A rumble from deep within the Emporium filled the air, and the corridor groaned. Daniel leaned on the walls until the movement had subsided.

And then all was still once more, save for the juddering and quaking of a nearby door, and a distant rumble from beyond. Sharpe stepped forward and threw open the door. Whatever Wonder had lain beyond was now impossible to tell. All that remained was a room filled with wreckage, with twisted metal and darkness and a spreading silence.

"What's happening?" asked Daniel.

Sharpe closed the door. He rubbed the stubble of his chin. "There is so much raw magic in this place ... so much untamed imagination. It all requires an anchor, something – or someone – to keep it under control. Lucien is that anchor." At this, Sharpe touched the walls, shook his head. "But it seems he no longer has the strength."

"Mr Silver isn't controlling it any more?"

"Either he has already lost his grip, or it is slipping quickly away," said Sharpe. "The Emporium is beginning to rip at the seams. Some areas will be affected more than others to begin with, like diseased organs in a body. This is obviously one of them."

"How long can it last without him?" There was desperation in Daniel's voice. He hadn't been part of the Emporium for very long, but he felt as if it had been a part of him forever. Like it had been waiting for him, calling to him his entire life.

"I don't know," said Sharpe. "Hard to tell with this much energy swilling around. Maybe days, maybe weeks, or months. However long, it won't be pleasant."

"*Days?*" said Daniel.

Sharpe gave a shrug. "As I say, I can't be sure." A pause. The corners of his mouth creased. "I wonder. Is it possible?"

"What?" said Daniel. "Is what possible?"

Sharpe waved a hand. "Oh, just thinking aloud," he said. "I'm wondering … what would happen if we tried to use Lucien's book to find him?"

Daniel's hand touched the cover through his jacket.

"Mr Silver told me not to," he said. "And after what happened last time—"

"You're forgetting the circumstances, boy," said Sharpe. He sounded different, hungry somehow. "I'm sure Lucien will understand. It's an emergency after all. And you aren't alone, are you? You have me to help. This might be our best chance of finding Lucien. *Your* best chance to save your friends. All you have to do is create a door that'll lead us straight to Lucien."

Daniel brought out the book and stared at the battered cover. His fingers drummed on the leather. Was Sharpe right? Was it different this time? Maybe he *could* justify breaking Mr Silver's rules in a desperate situation like this.

At last, he said, "You're right. It's the best chance we've got. I'll do it."

CHAPTER 22

HANDS IN THE DARKNESS

"I really hope this wasn't a mistake."

Daniel stood so close to the new doorway that his nose almost touched the cold black surface. His heart banged in his chest. If Sharpe's plan was a success, then Mr Silver might be just the other side of the door.

"Something wrong?" Sharpe stood a few metres behind, hands grasping his cane tight. He sounded impatient.

"I'm just wondering what we're going to find," said Daniel, recalling the last time he broke the rules. "Even if it has worked, what if we walk through to find him hurt … or worse?"

Sharpe stepped forward and reached out an arm. For a moment, Daniel thought he was going to place a hand on his shoulder, to tell him not to worry and that Silver would surely be fine. But the hand passed him by, and instead gripped the handle of the door. The click of the latch sounded like a gunshot in the hush. The door crept open.

Daniel did not have time to scream.

Hundreds of emaciated, wrinkled hands crowded the doorway, reaching and grabbing at him, pulling him forward by the neck and the hair and ears, by the clothes. He could see no faces, no bodies, as he fought them. There were only shrunken, withered fingers. They surrounded him now; he was almost through the doorway, enveloped, suffocating. Fingers covered his mouth and nose. Perhaps he would die here. He closed his eyes, kicked and scratched and bit. A bony hand grabbed his head, twisted him around, pulled him further into the tangled mass.

And then Daniel heard a voice, filling his head to bursting.

"Leave," it said in a whisper that ran right through him. "Leave us."

Slowly, the hands released Daniel, and he wriggled and squirmed, feeling less crushing pressure, fewer cold grips. Another hand grabbed his own, this one warm, and he was heaved forwards.

He landed on the cold Emporium floor on his hands and knees, gasping, clutching his throat.

"The book! Do you still have the book?" Sharpe stood over him, his eyes bulging.

Daniel felt for his pocket. His shaking fingers touched upon the book. He nodded.

Sharpe spun away towards the open door, where hundreds of hands reached and clawed and grasped at the air. He grabbed the door, tried to pull it shut, but the hands refused, fought against him. Sharpe did not give up. He opened his mouth and yelled, a guttural scream from the depths of his belly. He pulled so hard that angry veins appeared on his neck and his forehead. Slowly, the door began to close, until the latch clicked, and Sharpe collapsed against the wood, holding it shut with all of his weight and strength.

"Get rid of it!" he yelled at Daniel.

The words shook Daniel from his daze. He reached into his pocket, pulled out the book and found the right page. Tearing it from the book, he ran to the nearest flickering lamp, and held the paper to the flame, where it turned to glowing ash and scattered.

The cracked black bricks around the door closed in, swivelling and shifting into place, multiplying until the doorway was blocked, the door gone. Sharpe leaned against the wall, panting.

"What did you do?" he said.

"Only what you asked me to," said Daniel. He stared at the book in his shaking hands, and at the place on the wall where the door had been. He tried to figure out what had gone wrong. Last time he'd written in the book without permission, Mr Silver had explained that there was a *reason* things had gone out of control: in trying to bring back his parents from the dead, Daniel had crossed an impossible and dangerous line. This time he'd attempted no such thing, only a simple doorway leading to Mr Silver.

"Maybe he doesn't want us to find him," he said, and his eyes widened as the idea struck him properly.

Sharpe gave him a quizzical look. "What are you talking about?"

"I heard a voice in that room. 'Leave us,' it said. I think what just happened was a warning from Mr Silver. A message. He was telling us not to come looking for him."

Sharpe straightened up, and dusted off his suit.

"I'm growing tired of these games," he said, and his voice was cold and sharp. Then he brushed past Daniel and walked away, his cane clicking on the floor.

As Daniel watched Sharpe go, something troubled him: he'd almost been eaten by a door, yet all Sharpe seemed to be worried about was whether the *Book of Wonders* was safe. In fact, every time Sharpe saw the book his eyes would shine and a strange look would creep over his face.

Daniel stowed the book back in his pocket, let his hand rest on it. Perhaps he was imagining things.

Sharpe had saved his life twice now, after all. The stress of the crumbling Emporium and of Mr Silver's disappearance might be taking its toll. He hoped so.

All the same, Ellie had been right. Sharpe was Daniel's responsibility.

From now on he'd watch his every move.

CHAPTER 23

CREATION

Edinburgh, June 1896

A pair of well-worn grey shoes stepped from the train carriage onto the platform of Edinburgh's Waverley Station. Lucien Silver had come home.

His handsome face was now a little more lived-in. The hair was a tangle of wild waves, the chin dotted with dark stubble.

He stayed for a few days in a modest hotel near the centre of the city. He walked the wide streets, occasionally stumbling upon a building or a point of view that would spark hazy memories of rare trips outside the walls of Castlefoot Home for Lost Boys.

On his third day, Lucien discovered an empty

building in one of Edinburgh's narrow backstreets. He asked around, learning that the shop belonged to an elderly baker who had retired and left it empty.

On the morning of Lucien's fourth day back in Edinburgh, word of something remarkable began to spread. The old baker's shop was gone. It had been replaced (overnight, it seemed) with a grand building made of sparkling black stone. An Emporium of some sort, though nobody was exactly sure what it might sell.

Some described the place as a living dream. Some said that the young man who ran the shop must be a genius, an illusionist with no equal, for inside the shop they had seen Wonders beyond belief, or science, or reason.

Word of mouth is a magic of its own. Many that lived in the city, or nearby, became bewitched, returning again and again, sometimes every day. When journalists and writers picked up on the story, a new wave of patrons descended on Edinburgh, eager to see the work of the remarkable young man they'd read about. They came from Glasgow and Newcastle, Liverpool and London and beyond. None were disappointed.

And nobody ever suspected that the magic was real.

Lucien lined his pockets with more money than he ever imagined. He barely slept. His days were spent running the Emporium, his nights imagining new Wonders to capture the imagination of the public.

With every stroke of the pen he would remember Vindictus Sharpe's cold words in the graveyard, words that fuelled his every move: *"You will never be better than me. I rescued you from the gutter, and that is where I expect you to return…"*

Lucien had no intention of ever returning to the gutter. He wished beyond anything that one day Sharpe would walk through the doors. Then he would laugh in his face, and Sharpe would be forced to admit the cleverness of Lucien's magic.

In the meantime, the Nowhere Emporium was open for business.

Yes indeed.

And business was booming.

CHAPTER 24

RESCUE

The Emporium's decay was speeding up. The cracks in the walls grew, and chunks of stone began to break away. The once shining black brick seemed dull and lifeless. Lamps had flickered out, and could not be relit. Doors began to lock without explanation. A strange illness was beginning to strike the staff; they became weak and fevered.

Daniel felt it too; his connection with the shop was fading. There were frightening moments when he found himself lost and confused, only for his knowledge to return.

Several times, Sharpe left the Emporium at night, complaining that he needed to eat – though Daniel had never seen anything pass his lips except whisky. When

Sharpe was gone, Daniel sometimes found himself hoping that he wouldn't come back. The uneasy feeling in his gut was getting stronger, and the more time he spent with the magician, the more positively Daniel felt he was hiding something.

One night, when Sharpe was out, Daniel checked in on his friends.

Caleb was revelling in his role as organiser. Every day he'd been sending out groups of vendors and performers to the increasingly dangerous far reaches of the Emporium. There were phantom sightings and false alarms, but no Mr Silver.

And no Ellie.

"We've discovered a long-lost part of the Emporium," Caleb told Daniel. "A secret tunnel! It'll take days to properly search it, and Ellie has gone with the expedition."

"They won't find him," said Daniel, and he told Caleb about his attempt to write in the book, and the door that almost ate him.

"So you think Silver is alive?" said Caleb. "That's great news!"

"Maybe," said Daniel, "but why doesn't he want anyone to find him? What's he doing? What's he so scared of?"

"We should call off the search parties," said Caleb.

"Agreed," said Daniel, and the thought that Ellie would finally be coming back cheered him. He missed her. He missed how she made him happy and angry and want to tear his hair out all at the same time. And he had been terrified that something would happen to her, that she'd be caught in one of the crumbling Wonders as it self-destructed. He hoped she'd be able to help him work out what was going on. And just having her around would make him less nervous about spending time with Sharpe.

Daniel heard the screams for help on a Monday morning.

He followed the noise, up and around, and found a corridor half caved-in, blocked by fallen chunks of roof and wall.

The muffled ring of shattering glass spilled from a warped, twisted door near the blockage.

The screams grew louder, more desperate.

Daniel ran to the door and tried to open it, but it was bent and jammed. He kicked at the handle, again and again, until at last the door burst open, revealing a palace made entirely of glass. It was beautiful. It was delicate and shimmering. And it was falling apart. Everywhere the glass was marked by crawling, inching cracks. The sound of glass popping and shattering was all around. As Daniel followed the screams, long shards fell inches from him, exploding on the floor in countless sparkling fragments. He pressed onward, dodging and weaving, until he ducked under a doorway, entering a grand dining room.

His heart almost stopped. Anja was lying over a glass table. Her eyes were shut. A pool of black liquid, like ink, had formed around her and was dripping from the table to the floor. Stuck deep in her shoulder was a glass blade as long as Daniel's arm.

"Anja! Anja, I'm here! It's Daniel. Can you hear me?"

She didn't move, didn't acknowledge him in any way. Daniel struggled to drape her over his shoulder. Then he began to pull her away, her limp feet dragging on the floor as the dining room crashed down around them. Out into the main hall, and he gathered pace. But white-hot pain flashed in his foot, and he dropped to the ground, Anja landing awkwardly on top of him. Daniel knew his foot was bleeding; he could feel the hot blood pouring from the wound. He also knew if he didn't get Anja out they'd both be stuck many times over with razor-sharp glass. As the shattering roar became unbearable, he struggled up and dragged Anja through the door, jamming it shut behind.

"Help! Somebody help!"

"Daniel!"

Vindictus Sharpe sped towards them, blue eyes almost glowing in the dim light.

"Mr Sharpe! You've got to help her! Oh, she can't die. Please don't let her die!"

Sharpe brushed Daniel aside, crouched low over Anja. He felt her throat.

"She's alive."

Daniel slumped to the floor in relief. Sharpe pulled the glass shard from Anja's shoulder and a jet of black spurted high into the air. Then Sharpe's eyes closed and he muttered under his breath, his fingers tracing the outline of the deep gash. The pouring liquid slowed. Then it stopped. Torn skin began to knit together until nothing remained but the thinnest of scars.

Sharpe turned his attention to Daniel.

"This will hurt. Close your eyes."

Daniel sat by the fire sipping hot tea to steady his nerves as he waited for Sharpe to return. When the big man swept through the curtain from the labyrinth of corridors, Daniel leapt up.

"What happened? Will Anja be OK?"

Sharpe removed his coat, hung it near the door, and took a silver flask from the pocket, swallowing a mouthful of the liquid inside.

"She should recover. But even then, there's every chance she'll catch the sickness that's spreading through the staff. Without Lucien they are rotting away, just like the Emporium. It's not blood inside them. It's ink."

Daniel pushed his palm against the cool glass of the window. Hot tears gathered in his eyes. Why was it that everything he loved, or cared about, or depended on went away in the end? What was wrong with him?

Sharp said, "I don't believe there's much time left." His big hands were pressed together, like he was praying. "We need to find Lucien. Now."

Daniel shook his head. "I've been thinking. Mr Silver has always done what's best for this place. Why would he stop now? If I'm right, and he doesn't want to be found, then there must be a reason. I trust him."

"Do you trust him enough to die here if you're wrong?" said Sharpe. "Look … Lucien is *ill*. You said so yourself. He might not be thinking clearly. He might have gone mad for all we know. If we don't find him, I promise you, everything in this shop, including your friends, will be gone. And you're going to have to start thinking about life outside the Emporium again."

Daniel stared desperately.

"I don't want to leave."

"Then help me!"

"How?"

Sharpe let out a deep sigh.

"I know Lucien better than anyone. I know how

his mind works. Perhaps if I were to study the *Book of Wonders*, I might find something that you have missed. The tiniest clue can make all the difference."

Daniel reached for his pocket. He brought the book out and stared at the battered cover. He was tired, and frightened, and confused. Could Sharpe be right? Was it possible Mr Silver was losing his mind?

"It is your decision," said Sharpe. "If you do not wish me to have the book, I understand." He pointed to the gold watch on his wrist. "But time is running out. And consider this: how would you feel if the Emporium slipped away and you knew that you had not done *everything* in your power to save it? To save your friends?"

Daniel's hand trembled as he clutched the book. Sharpe was right: how could he ignore any chance, no matter how small, of saving his home and the people who had filled his life with magic?

He held out the *Book of Wonders*.

Sharpe stared at it. He licked his lips, reached out hungry fingers. Just like that, the *Book of Wonders* was gone, nestling in Sharpe's hands.

"How can I help?" Daniel asked.

Sharpe tore his eyes from the book.

"Mmm? Oh … I insist on doing this alone, boy. I won't achieve much with you staring over my shoulder. Besides, you've been through quite an ordeal today. It's best if you rest."

As Sharpe spoke, Daniel's eyelids grew heavy, and tiredness weighed upon his shoulders. "You'll tell me if you find anything?" he managed to say through a yawn as he slumped into a dusty old armchair near the window.

Sharpe flashed those white teeth.

"If I find what I am looking for, boy, you will know about it. Believe me."

And with that he turned and swept away through the curtain.

Daniel watched after him. Somewhere in the back of his head, something was screaming out at him. But he did not care any more. Tiredness wrapped around him, suffocating the world, and he curled up in the deep chair and closed his eyes.

CHAPTER 25

THE NOTHINGNESS

Daniel woke with a start. Several of the clocks on the walls displayed the date as well as the time, and they told him that he'd slept through an entire day. It was strange how tiredness had crept over him just as he'd given the book to Sharpe…

Daniel's hand touched the empty pocket. He thought of the book. Usually, when he wished to find anything in the Emporium – an object or a place – he would simply hold a picture of it in his mind and he would know in an instant where it could be located. But now, when he pictured the *Book of Wonders*, he could see nothing. There was a blind spot in his vision, like static interference, and it was not being caused by the weakening Emporium. The only explanation was that Sharpe was blocking him, purposely keeping him at arm's length. And why would he do that? What did he have to hide?

Sharpe had made everything seem so hopeless, made Daniel think handing over the *Book of Wonders* was the only option left. But now his head was clear, Daniel was starting to realise the enormity of his mistake.

In half a beat he was through the curtain, and right away it was obvious that something had changed. Looking at the decaying great hall of stairways was like visiting some ancient ruin, or the site of a disaster. The stairs were worn and broken. Many of the flickering torches had died, casting the corridors in cold shadow and gloom. The air was tinged with the taste of smoke, and thick dust, and of something sour and metallic. In the day Daniel had been asleep, the Emporium's disease had progressed rapidly.

A terrible thought knocked the wind from him: the Nowhere Hotel! Would it still be standing? Were his friends OK?

Sprinting through the dark, Daniel found his path blocked time and again by the debris of collapsed corridors. A Wonder called the Shipwreck had burst open, flooding several passages with waist-deep water, full of colourful fish.

The door to the Nowhere Hotel was, like many of the other Wonders, cracked and warped. As soon as

Daniel saw it he knew something bad had happened inside. The revolving door deposited him in the lobby, which had been so vibrant and grand the last time he visited. Now it was silent. Lights flickered on and off, and columns of black marble were crumbling. There were fissures in the floor and places where the ceiling had collapsed.

"Hello?" said Daniel, flinching at the sound of his own voice. There was no answer. He did not want to go any further. He was scared, both of the lonely gloom and of what might have happened to his friends. But his friends were exactly the reason he had to go on. Ellie lived in this place and it was impossible for her to escape. What if she was trapped somewhere? What if she was hurt? But where? Which room was hers? Where should he begin his search?

"Caleb's room!" he said to himself. "What number was it? What number, what number, what number … 108! It was 108!"

He ran to the elevator, punched the button. Nothing happened. "Of course it isn't working," said Daniel to the Emporium. "Why make things easy for me?" He kicked the wall, and a chunk of black marble broke off and thudded to his feet.

The stairs were narrow and steep, all bare concrete and flickering strip lights, and as Daniel climbed floor after floor the Nowhere Hotel creaked and groaned around him. He knew it could all fall apart at any moment, knew that this Wonder could disappear from existence as easily as any of the others. But he pushed through the fear.

When he reached the tenth floor his legs and lungs were burning.

Keep going. Keep going.

Through the door, he took a slow step forward, and another, and then he froze. A metre or two in front of him, where there should have been floor and walls, should have been the door to Caleb's room, should have been something, anything ... there was nothing.

The walls came to a jagged stop, like some monster had bitten the corridor in half. The floor stopped suddenly, a lip of ragged black carpet; and beyond, opening up in every direction, was a darkness that went on forever. Daniel stared into the black, saw no wreckage, no light, no sign that anything at all had ever existed. He imagined stepping off the edge, falling into that nothingness, tumbling forever, losing all memory of who he was or how long he'd been there, until he became part of the nothing too, part of the fabric of the darkness. Lost.

Was Caleb lost? Anja? Had the nothing swallowed Ellie?

He tore one foot from the floor and stepped back. A deep rumble filled the place, like the breath of a sleeping giant. A small section of floor and wall broke off and spun away into the nothing as the world lurched violently forwards, throwing Daniel onto the carpet. He landed with a thud, knocking the wind from his body, and rolled and skidded and bumped out of control towards an unimaginable fall. He threw out a desperate hand. His fingers found the ragged edge of the black carpet, and he clung on and managed to stop himself going all the way over. His lower body was now hanging out over the edge of the abyss. His grip tightened desperately on the carpet, but the weight of him was beginning to fray the material and he watched in helpless horror as the carpet ripped slowly, slowly, and finally snapped. He fell back with a sickening jerk—

A hand, huge and warm, wrapped around his wrist, hoisted him high. He was slung over a wide shoulder, and he watched, blinking the sweat from his eyes, as the remainder of the floor began breaking and crumbling like dry cake.

I'm dead, he thought.

The person who was carrying him leapt back, just as the floor collapsed completely, and for a moment Daniel felt like he was back in the Leap of Faith, soaring through the sky. Then they landed, and rolled, and tumbled, and Daniel was flung against something hard and cold.

"Are you all right?"

Daniel rubbed his head and face. There was a smear of fresh blood on his hand. Standing over him, looking down with a concerned expression, was Caleb. They were back in the stairwell, but the nothing was spreading. The door to the tenth floor was being swallowed up, and the walls of the stairwell were already beginning to crack.

Daniel threw his arms around Caleb. "You saved my life!" he said. "Where is everyone? Is Ellie all right?"

"Let's talk on the move," said Caleb. "The further we are from the edge, the better."

Daniel noticed Caleb flinch as they descended the stairs. He seemed to be favouring one of his arms, holding it tight to his body. There was something else – something missing.

"Where's Mr Bobo?" Daniel had never seen Caleb without his ragged, no-eyed teddy bear.

Caleb's lip trembled. "He didn't make it," he said in a low, sad voice. "You saw. My room is gone. Bobo was inside when it … when it was swallowed by the dark." He took a handkerchief from his pocket and blew his nose. When he lowered the hanky, a drop of ink trickled from his nostril. He wiped his nose with his hand, and stared at the black smear on his skin.

"I suppose I should have expected it eventually," he said with a sad sigh. "We're all just characters in Silver's book, and we'll fade to nothing without him … just like the Emporium. Half of us were wiped out when the hotel began to crumble. Most of the survivors are dying of illness. It seems I can now count myself in that category."

"Anja?" said Daniel. "Did she make it?"

"She survived," said Caleb. "She is still recovering from her injuries." He smiled, and placed a massive hand on Daniel's shoulder. "I heard you saved her. Everyone knows, Daniel Holmes, and we thank you. We are in your debt forever."

"The way things are going there won't be time for tomorrow, never mind forever," said Daniel. "Where are the rest of the staff?"

"Silver made a hospital wing years ago," said Caleb. "In case anything ever happened to his customers. It has never been used until now. Thankfully it's still in one piece. For the moment at least." He let out a wheeze, wiped inky blood from the corner of his mouth. He waved away Daniel's concerned look. "There's nothing can be done for the ill. We can only make them as comfortable as possible."

"And Ellie?" asked Daniel. "Have you seen her?"

Caleb shook his head.

"Her search party was due to be the last back. They haven't returned yet."

"She's still out there?" Daniel leaned against the wall and put his face in his hands.

Caleb sighed. "She's tough," he said. "I'm sure she'll make it back." He paused to wipe his nose again, and then went on. "There is something I think you should know. Ellie doesn't have a condition; there's no magical disease that stops her from leaving the shop. It's Mr Silver who's keeping her here."

"What? You mean she's his prisoner?"

"He loves her very much," said Caleb. "But he says Ellie must stay for her own protection. He will not tell her exactly what she needs protecting from. Ellie thinks he is being selfish. She believes Mr Silver keeps her in the shop because he doesn't want to be alone. So, you can see why she's so desperate. Not only is her father missing, but he is the only one who can release her from this place. She is trapped in a crumbling tomb."

They reached the lobby, the fire-eater and the boy, and stood face to face at the exit.

"You are not carrying the *Book of Wonders*," said Caleb, indicating Daniel's empty inside pocket. "I can sense when it is close by. It's the first time I've seen you without it since Silver disappeared." He began to cough wildly, and leaned on the wall, wiping more inky blood from his face.

"I have to go," said Daniel, worry swelling in his chest. He didn't dare confess that he'd given the book away. "Try to look after the others, and yourself. And if you see Ellie please tell her I'm so sorry and I need her help. I'll see you soon."

He turned away, wondering if he'd ever see the fire-breather again, and began to walk the lonely corridors in search of Vindictus Sharpe and the *Book of Wonders*.

CHAPTER 26

AN UNEXPECTED VISITOR

Edinburgh, June 1897

Lucien Silver's Emporium was the talk of Edinburgh, and far beyond. There were days when the shop was so busy that he barely remembered a face, the stream of customers becoming a blur of smiles and compliments.

But on the first anniversary of the Emporium's opening, Lucien was introduced to a face he would never forget.

He had placed an advertisement in each of the city newspapers, announcing that entry to the Emporium would be free. On the day itself, Silver sat at his desk near the red velvet curtain, nodding to passing customers. Many of them commented that it seemed impossible that so many wondrous rooms could exist in a stick-thin little shop.

Near the end of the day, someone approached the desk. At first, Lucien did not look up from his book, but then he heard a familiar voice, deep and firm and cold.

"Hello, Lucien."

Vindictus Sharpe had not aged a day since their last encounter in the rainy Edinburgh graveyard. This did not shock Lucien. In his travels before he settled back in Edinburgh, he had discovered layers of magic that were hidden to all but a select few, magic that could unlock the mysteries of life and time and the universe. He was more certain now than ever that he knew the secret to Vindictus Sharpe's long life. Sharpe was stealing the future from innocent people; stealing time and adding it to his own life.

Lucien stood. He had been waiting for this moment for a long, long time; to be able to rub his success in Sharpe's face, to show him how wrong he'd been. He had actually stayed awake at night imagining exactly what he'd say if they ever crossed paths again.

This was the chance.

Something shifted behind Sharpe. He moved aside, and Lucien's eyes met those of a second person.

All thoughts of Sharpe were lost.

The young woman was perhaps a year or two younger than Lucien. Her skin was fair and freckled, and her hair fell in tumbling red curls over her shoulders.

"This is Michelle, my daughter," said Sharpe.

Michelle held out a porcelain hand, and Lucien kissed it. As his lips touched her skin, the air in the room seemed to shiver and crackle.

Lucien pulled at his necktie. "Pleasure to meet you. I … I don't recall your father ever mentioning a daughter."

Sharpe sat on the edge of the desk and began examining one of Lucien's fountain pens. "There were a great many things I did not mention. Michelle has been in boarding school most of her life. I travel the world, and that is no way for a young girl to grow up."

Lucien nodded. He felt his gaze drawn back to Michelle.

"Well, what can I do for you?" he asked. "What brings you to Edinburgh?"

"Business," said Sharpe. "I am booked to perform in Edinburgh for one month. Word of your work has reached me from the magic committee." At this he glanced around the shop. "I could not resist stopping by for a peek."

Lucien smiled. "Then a peek you shall have. Miss Sharpe, would you care for a tour of my Emporium?"

Michelle Sharpe's blue eyes met Lucien Silver's thunder-grey ones. She smiled a shy smile. "I'd like that very much, Mr Silver," she said.

And so Lucien led the way, taking great delight in Michelle's amazement, using every opportunity to remind Sharpe how the idea for the Emporium was born in the very same notes he had dismissed as nonsense.

Two hours later, when the tour was complete, Lucien watched Sharpe and his daughter stride down the narrow street.

He was sure of two things.

Number one: he had surpassed Sharpe in every possible way. More importantly, Sharpe was aware of this fact, and it would eat away at his insides like an infestation of maggots. This thought made Lucien very happy.

Number two: Michelle Sharpe was nothing like her father. She was enchanting and warm, and Lucien knew that he must, no matter what it took, see her again.

His wish was granted the next day.

Michelle returned to the Emporium, and this time she was not with her father.

"I had to see it all again," she confessed. "It is remarkable, and impossible. I couldn't stop thinking of you or your Emporium when I left."

They walked the shop's ever-growing number of corridors, Michelle laughing in delight when rain began to fall in one of the passageways. Lucien produced a black umbrella seemingly from nowhere and held it over her head.

The day passed in a haze of shy laughter.

As she left, Michelle gave him a lopsided smile. "I

don't think my father likes you very much."

Lucien breathed in her words. "The feeling is mutual," he said.

"You're not scared of him the way everyone else is, are you?" Michelle said.

"No. Being frightened of him is only giving him what he wants."

Michelle beamed at him. Then she did something he had not been expecting. She leaned in, pressing her lips gently against his mouth.

When the kiss was over, Lucien stumbled back a step, ran flustered hands through his tangled hair. "What … er … what was that for?"

But she only smiled and turned away, through the door to the cool Edinburgh sunshine. Lucien watched her, his face pressed against the glass of the shop window, until she turned the corner and was gone.

Lucien and Michelle spent every day of the following month together, hidden away from the world. Each night, he would create a new Wonder to bewitch her. The sound of her laughter was intoxicating, and the touch of her lips a drug to which he soon became addicted.

Beat by beat, Michelle Sharpe was stealing Lucien Silver's heart.

If only he had known what was next on her list.

CHAPTER 27

THE TRUTH

Daniel's worry was turning to cold panic. He had rushed back to the shop front to look for Sharpe, but he wasn't there. He prayed that all of this was a misunderstanding, that Sharpe simply wanted privacy to study each page in his quest to find Mr Silver.

But as Daniel paced anxiously around the dusty room he grew more certain that Ellie had been right, that there was something off about Sharpe. He began to move the pieces around in his mind, struggling to fit them together: Sharpe had shown up only days after Silver's disappearance; there was a hungry look in his eyes every time he caught sight of the *Book of Wonders*; Daniel had fallen into a deep sleep after handing him the book and hadn't seen or heard from him since...

Just like that, the puzzle clicked together.

If the wrong person got hold of it, the *Book of Wonders* could be used to *hurt* the Emporium just as easily as help it. It couldn't be a coincidence, could it? Sharpe had the book, and everything was crumbling so much faster. Somehow, his presence was speeding things up, causing more damage.

And there was one room where that damage could be fatal.

Daniel ran and ran, his legs and lungs pleading for rest. He needed to know if he was right about Sharpe. And he now knew beyond doubt he had to get the *Book of Wonders* back. Without it, everything Mr Silver had ever created would be lost.

But as he made his way deeper into the corridors, his mind clouded, and he became confused, losing all sense of direction. His connection with the shop was fading again.

"Not now. Please!"

A twist and a turn, leaping down a staircase three steps at a time, and another and another, until one of the stairs crumbled beneath him, and he rolled the final few steps and landed with an awkward slap on the floor.

Daniel's arm throbbed. He fought back the tears, clenching his fists.

A flutter of wings. A flash of silver.

Something clipped Daniel's shoulder, and landed with a graceful hop beside him. The silver magpie twitched its head to one side, observed him for a few seconds. Then it called out again, and almost immediately the second bird appeared, gliding in a circle over Daniel's head and corkscrewing down to land on his shoulder. It pecked at his ear.

Daniel tried to wave it away.

"Beat it. I'm not in the mood."

The pecking continued. The first bird, the one at Daniel's side, called out again, and flew off down a dark corridor. Before he could blink, the bird was back, this time landing on his head and pecking at his skull as if trying to open a tough nut.

Daniel let out a laugh.

"You can show me the way!" he said, scrambling up. "Come on, we need to get to the Fountain."

The birds were clearly agitated as they flew. Daniel found it difficult to keep up, and every so often they'd swoop down and nip him on the ear, or pull at his hair with sharp beaks. They led him to the great hall of staircases, down and down, to a crumbling corridor where frost was gathering on the black stone. Daniel rubbed his hands together as he breathed winter morning air. A door was ajar, letting a blade of sunlight into the darkness. Daniel knew where he was, knew that he had visited this place before when he was new to the Emporium. He

paused at the entrance, reached out and traced the
frost-covered golden letters:

With a push the door was fully open, and Daniel
stood once again on the surface of a frozen pond
surrounded by woodland, hot breath rising from his
mouth. Everything was as he remembered: the crisp
air, the endless stretch of blue sky.

And then he saw the broken mountain of stone
that lay in the centre of the pond where the fountain
should have been.

Daniel hurried out across the pond, his feet
crunching in the frost. He picked up a piece of what
had once been the fountain and tossed it from hand
to hand. There was no sign at all of the silvery liquid,
the imagination that Mr Silver had described as the
lifeblood of the Emporium. Part of the outer bowl
remained intact, though there were sharp fragments
of rock jutting out here and there, one of them
smeared with a thin red liquid. Blood.

"A sorry sight, don't you think?"

Vindictus Sharpe stood a few metres away, on the
opposite side of the fountain, his hands behind his
back. He had not been there a moment ago.

"Why have you come?" he said. "Didn't I ask for time to study the book alone?"

"Things have changed," said Daniel. "I think I made a mistake."

A pause. He took a long breath.

"I'd like the *Book of Wonders* back, please."

Sharpe raised a silver eyebrow.

"You'd … like it back?"

"Yes. It wasn't really mine to give away. You can still study it, but I'd like to be there when you do."

A thin smile crossed Sharpe's lips. "If it was not yours to give away," he said, "then it is certainly not yours to take back."

Daniel stared into the cold blue eyes. An alarm bell was ringing in his head, telling him he'd been right, that Sharpe was dangerous. He glanced again at the fountain, at the sharp point of stone smeared with blood.

"Whose blood is that?"

Sharpe hesitated. Then he brought his hands from behind his back. They were clutching the *Book of Wonders*, and they were covered in cuts and scrapes.

Daniel took a half-step back. He wanted to run, but he couldn't. This was his mess, his mistake.

Sharpe flashed a smile like a knife. "You've caught me red-handed, as it were. To tell the truth, I am growing tired of the act. I have no intention of returning the book to you, Daniel. In fact, the only reason I allowed you to hold on to it for so long was that I thought you might lead me to Lucien."

Daniel stared at the *Book of Wonders* in Sharpe's big hands.

"I don't get it ... wrecking the fountain ... you're speeding things up, killing the Emporium. Why?"

"Back when we were walking together," said Sharpe, "you asked me what Lucien was running from. What could possibly frighten him enough that he spent his whole life looking over his shoulder, always ready to flee to the next town, the next city, the next window in time..." Sharpe brushed a hand over his neat silver hair, ran his fingers over his moustache. "The answer, boy, is that Lucien Silver was running – is still running – from me."

Daniel heard the words, but he could not make sense of them.

"Why?"

Sharpe moistened his lips with his tongue. He lifted up the *Book of Wonders*.

"The book?" said Daniel. "That's what all of this is about? So if you've got it, why are you still here? Why haven't you just taken it away?"

"It's not quite as simple as that. A magician cannot steal a magical object from another of his kind. The bond between the creation and the creator is too intense. If I walk out of here with the book, it will not work for me as fully as I desire. No, for the *Book of Wonders* to truly be mine, I must either win it from Lucien, or he must pass it to me with his blessing. The latter is never going to happen. So I have no choice but to take the book through more … aggressive measures.

"I have been chasing for many years, boy, and each time I come close, each time I can feel the book, smell it, Lucien wriggles away. Not this time. Something is different. He is weak. I found him easily." At this Sharpe spat on the frost. "You can see how he has reacted, running away like the weasel he has always been."

"You hoped I'd lead you to him," Daniel said, "so you could … what? Kill him?"

Sharpe smiled an affable smile. "That's about the size of it," he said. "But seeing as you failed in spectacular fashion to locate him, I turned to other means. I knew that there must be a weakness somewhere in the Emporium, and that I could find it in the book." He opened his arms. "And here we are. The Fountain. Lucien has been relying on the imagination of his customers to keep the place running. He is weaker than I thought. He no longer has any customers. And now that the fountain is no more, the Emporium will crumble much more quickly.

"Lucien has a choice. He can either stay in his hole like a rodent and die with this place, or he can come out, come out, wherever he is, and face me. Either way, the *Book of Wonders* will be mine." He nodded to

Daniel. "You have talent, a connection with the book that could be very useful. The end of the Emporium need not be the end of your journey. I could help you become great."

"Help me like you helped Mr Silver?" said Daniel. "No thanks. I don't fancy a knife in the back."

Sharpe shrugged his wide shoulders and said, "Lucien has nobody to blame but himself. His actions, his cowardice, sealed his fate. The choice is yours. Stay here and wait for the Emporium to die. Go down with the ship. Or learn from the best, and open up a new world of possibilities."

Daniel returned the cold stare, trying with all of his might to hide the fear coursing through him. The enormity of his mistake was hitting him hard. *He* had invited Sharpe in. *He* had handed over the *Book of Wonders*.

Every cell in his body was telling him to turn and run.

But Daniel did not run away. He stepped forward.

"You ... you think I could be great?" he said.

Sharpe leaned his head a little to one side, as if sizing him up.

"I think that, together, we could discover secrets about the book that even Lucien does not know."

Daniel took another step forward, his heart thundering. His eyes flicked to the book, but only for half a second.

Just a little closer.

"How can the book have secrets from Mr Silver?" Daniel asked.

"Magic has its mysteries, my boy ... even for the best of us..."

From somewhere behind him, Daniel heard the call of a magpie.

Sharpe looked away only for a moment, but it was enough.

Daniel snatched the book from his hands and spun away through the frost towards the doorway. He didn't dare look back as he ran.

What next? Where to go? He almost tripped over his own feet. A few more steps ... just a few more...

A strong hand grabbed at his hair, snapped him backwards with such force that his feet left the frosted ground. When he landed, there was no time to react. Sharpe stood over him, sneering. He grabbed him again by the hair and dragged him up. Then, a look of mad fury on his face, Sharpe reared back and struck Daniel across the mouth.

The world blurred at the edges. Daniel stumbled to his knees, blood pooling in his mouth. Sharpe was stalking towards him like a big cat. He was enjoying himself. Daniel backed away, still on his knees.

"You'll never find him," he said, clutching the *Book of Wonders* to his chest. "Nobody will find him if he doesn't want to be found."

Sharpe nodded. "Then I'll wait," he said, "until this place falls apart and takes him with it. But I will win."

He raised his great hand again.

Daniel cringed, waiting for the next blow to arrive. But before he could connect, the magpies swooped down upon Sharpe, pecking at his eyes, crying out with chattering screeches.

Daniel knew that the birds were calling to him, *Run away! Take the book to safety!* But he was dazed, unable to do anything but watch Sharpe flail and curse.

Sharpe, who had been staggering backwards, grabbed one of the magpies as it arrowed towards his face. It wriggled and called out as he tightened his grip around it and slammed it to the ground with a sickening crack. Then he lifted his foot and brought it down with all of his strength and weight, crushing the delicate metal bird beneath the sole of his shining black shoe.

"No!" Daniel wanted to run at Sharpe, to jump at him and hurt him.

Sharpe looked up, dragging his gaze from the shimmering carcass of the magpie, and Daniel felt a jolt of ice in his spine.

The second magpie continued to attack, buying Daniel moments. He glanced at the book in his hands, turned, and began to run.

The frost was slippery beneath his feet as he dashed to the door. Before he was through, he heard Sharpe call out, "You can't hide forever, Daniel Holmes. Sooner or later, I will find you, and when I do, I will take back my book! The only way I'll leave without it is in a coffin!"

CHAPTER 28

REUNITED

The wings of the surviving magpie flashed in the darkness as Daniel raced through the passageways. His fingers gripped the *Book of Wonders* tight. He did not know or care where the bird was leading him, so long as it was away from Sharpe.

Everything seemed darker than before; the shadows were deeper and the silence suffocating. Again and again Daniel thought he saw something shifting in the gloom; he imagined Sharpe posing as a statue, detaching from the shadows to make a grab for the book.

What now? What could be done to stop a madman? How much time was there to save the Emporium now that the fountain was gone? And what could he do about it alone?

The sound of splashing from around the next corner stopped Daniel dead. Steep steps led to a flooded passageway. The water was waist-deep. Shattered diamonds of light sparkled on the dark surface, cast from the lamps lining the walls, some of which were still lit. A lone figure was wading through the water towards him.

"Ha ha! Ellie!"

He felt such relief that he actually laughed out loud.

He crashed down the stairs, slipping under the surface for a moment, taking in an unpleasant gulp of salty water, which shot out of his nose as he coughed and spluttered.

"Ellie! It's me!"

Ellie, who had been staring into the water as she waded, looked up. Her eyes grew wide.

"Daniel!" she cried. "I've been looking all over for you since our search party got back. The place is in ruins! I've just come from the hospital. The staff are in a bad way. Caleb told me you'd rushed off." She paused, and stared at Daniel's bloodied face. "What happened to you?"

"There's so much to tell you," said Daniel. "I'm pretty sure your father is alive, and he's in the Emporium." Daniel told her about Sharpe's idea of using the book to find Silver, and how it had backfired. "I think it was a message," he said. "Your father doesn't want to be found."

"But he's alive!" said Ellie, hopping on the spot.

"Thank you, Daniel! I couldn't stop picturing him dying all alone in some dark corner." She hugged Daniel tight, and then she broke away, looking serious. "He's still ill, though, isn't he? The Emporium's falling apart. He can't hold it all together. So why doesn't he want us to find him?"

"It's not us he's hiding from, Ellie," said Daniel. "It's Sharpe. You were right about him all along. He's dangerous." Daniel took a deep breath. "He wants to kill your papa."

"He *what?*"

"Kill him, and steal the *Book of Wonders*. That's why he's here. He's been chasing Mr Silver for a long time. He's obsessed with the book! He'll do anything to have it. And the book won't work properly for him unless Mr Silver hands it over, or Sharpe beats him for it. It's the reason your father makes the Emporium move around so much – he's running away! I think that's why people from outside can't see you. It's your papa's way of protecting you. I'll bet it's the reason he won't let you leave the shop too. It's all to keep you safe from Sharpe."

Ellie's mouth moved wordlessly before she found her voice. "How do you know all this?"

"Sharpe told me so himself," said Daniel. And the story began to spill out of him: how the magpies had led him to the fountain; how he'd only just escaped with his life after stealing back the book; how one of the birds had not been so lucky.

Ellie's hand went to her mouth. "He wrecked the fountain? And he did that to you?" She pointed to Daniel's swollen lip. He could still taste the blood, and the saltwater nipped at the wound.

"I'm sorry," said Daniel. "I've messed everything up. I should never have let him in. All I ever wanted to do was help. I don't want to lose the Emporium, or Mr Silver, or you."

To his surprise, Ellie smiled her crooked smile.

"All that matters now is what we do next. We can still turn things around."

Daniel thought for a moment.

"If we can get rid of Sharpe," he said, "I reckon Mr Silver will come back."

"Why didn't Papa just stand up to him in the first place?"

Daniel knew what Ellie was thinking: that Mr Silver was a coward. He'd even thought the same himself at first.

"I don't think it's as simple as that. Your papa is weak. All the years of running the Emporium on his own have taken his strength away. I think he knew what was coming. He could sense Sharpe getting close, and he knew he wasn't strong enough to fight."

"That would explain the unicorn blood!" said Ellie. "It was desperation. A last attempt to get some of his strength back so that he could get rid of Sharpe."

"I think so," said Daniel. "Only something went wrong."

Ellie stroked the walls of the Emporium. "All these years I was sure he was keeping me in the shop so he wouldn't be lonely. I was always so angry at him."

"He's been protecting you. It's what they do, mums and dads."

"So what do we do?" said Ellie. "How can we get rid of Sharpe?"

"Everyone's got a weak spot," said Daniel thoughtfully. "We've got to find Sharpe's."

"But how? It's not like we can go and have a chat with him, is it? Get his life story over a nice cup of tea and some empire biscuits? He's dangerous!"

Life story…

The words echoed in Daniel's ears. He stared at the book, and began to flip through the pages, gathering speed as the idea properly formed. He heard Mr Silver's voice, far off on the horizon of his memory, from his very first lesson:

"I am a fan of stories. A collector. And there is no greater story than that of life. The Library of Souls holds on its many shelves the life story of everyone who has ever lived, everyone who will ever live."

Daniel stopped flipping. And there it was, staring back at him from the page in all of its dark, impossible glory. He flashed Ellie a clever smile.

"Who says we need to talk to Vindictus Sharpe to find out about his past?" he said. "This is the Nowhere Emporium, Ellie! Follow me."

CHAPTER 29

STOLEN

Edinburgh, July 1897

Michelle Sharpe giggled as she walked arm in arm with Lucien through the Emporium's growing number of corridors.

"What have you made for me this time?" she said. "It cannot be more beautiful than the Crystal Lake."

Lucien allowed himself a smile. He had created a new Wonder for Michelle every evening since they had met. One door led to a room made entirely from velvet-smooth chocolate. Another revealed a trek through the branches of an enormous Christmas tree, the aromas of roasting goose, spiced mincemeat and coal dust dancing in the air. It had taken him all evening to create the music mine — a vast cavern dotted with brightly coloured jewels that filled the air with beautiful melodies when they were plucked from the walls.

Lucien led her up a staircase to a solitary door.

"What is it?" she asked.

"Open it and find out," he said.

She reached for the handle, opened the door, and took a few hesitant steps into the room beyond.

"It's a garden," she said, barely able to speak through her amazement.

She was right. It was a garden, an overgrown wilderness of plants and flowers and trees. But every petal of every flower was made of fire. The world inside this impossible room was dark, lit only by the flicker from the flaming plants — blues and greens, reds, yellows, oranges.

"It's a fire garden," said Lucien. "I thought of you when I made it." He blushed as she turned and stared into his grey eyes.

"It's perfect," she whispered, and she began to wander around the garden.

Lucien watched. "You can touch the flames if you like. They won't burn."

Michelle reached up, touching her fingertips to the flaming blossom of a tree. Burning cinders fell to the ground, but her skin did not burn, and she laughed and stared around like a child.

"I have a surprise for you," Lucien said.

"Another surprise?"

He took her arm, led her through an archway of creeping ivy to a clearing surrounded by apple trees, each apple a ball of softly glowing fire. In the centre of the clearing sat a table loaded with food.

Lucien pulled out a chair for Michelle, keeping a keen eye on her as she sat.

"Is something the matter?" he asked. "You look a little sad."

She shook her head and smiled. "How could I be sad in a place like this?" Then she nodded to the feast. "May I try something? It all looks so delicious."

They began to eat, talking, as they loved to do, about running away together to desert islands and exotic cities where nobody would ever find them.

"Another drink," said Michelle, and she stood and poured two large glasses of wine, handing one to Lucien. She raised her glass. "To you, Lucien. And your wondrous Emporium."

Lucien clinked his glass against hers, and took a long sip of the wine.

He knew something was wrong at once. The garden began to spin and blur around him. A distant, echoing ring filled his head, and he saw nothing but blurred streaks of fire. He dropped his glass and it shattered on the grass, wine spilling like blood. Lucien grasped at the table as the corners of his vision faded to black.

The darkness began to close in around him. He was falling.

The last thing he saw before he hit the floor was Michelle, his broken vision fragmenting her face into many pieces. He reached out for her. She did nothing but watch.

Lucien was wakened by a slow, rhythmic pounding in his head. He screwed up his eyes to the surrounding fire-plants, grabbed hold of the table, and hoisted himself up. He did not know how long he had been unconscious. Every bit of him ached.

The table lay as he remembered: there were half finished plates of food and Michelle's wine glass lay empty beside her plate. Lucien's glass popped and snapped beneath his feet as he stumbled around.

Nothing made sense. What had happened? Where was Michelle?

The mist in his mind began to thin. A thought struck him. Dread choked him as he reached slowly into his coat pocket – to the place he kept the *Book of Wonders*.

His fingers found nothing but material.

His pocket was empty.

More to the point, someone had emptied it.

Michelle was gone. She had taken the *Book of Wonders* with her.

CHAPTER 30

THE LIBRARY OF SOULS

High in the Emporium's twisting corridors, Daniel and Ellie stood before a doorway in the midnight brick. Cracks were crawling along the walls even as they arrived.

The door swung open. Daniel felt a cool breath of air on his face, and a familiar, earthy scent lingered. The door led to a set of wooden steps. The steps opened up to a vast cavern filled with a calm black lake. All around, huge shapes stood in the water, monstrous shadows reaching towards a ceiling that might have been miles above.

A twinkle of light flickered somewhere in the gloom. Then another. And another. Gas lamps were glinting to life all around, blinking stars in the great darkness. The light was weak, but the darkness receded a little, and the giants in the water were visible for the first time.

They were bookcases.

When he had walked the streets of Manhattan, Daniel had often thought the tall buildings resembled great canyons of concrete and glass. The bookcases in this library were as tall as many of those buildings. Some of them stood in regimented rows, linked by bridges and stairways. Others took more interesting forms – spirals, pyramids and irregular mountains erupting from the black-mirrored surface.

A city of books, thought Daniel.

He stood with Ellie on a tiny island of wood, a platform no more than three metres square, black water lapping gently all around. Then, far off in the water, Daniel saw the soft glow of a lamp floating towards them. The speck became the shape of a boat, and on the boat stood a tall hooded figure in white robes.

The boat pulled up at the platform. The figure stepped from the boat onto the wooden floor.

"Welcome to the Library of Souls," it said, in a whispering voice that seemed to come from everywhere at once. Daniel wondered if the books themselves were speaking, and he shivered. The voice continued.

"Stories are precious. They are treasure. And the most precious story of all is that of life. Here, among these countless canals of ink, high in the bookcases, you shall find the story of everyone who has ever lived. Everyone who shall ever live. Past, present and future. Life and death. I will guide you to the tale that you seek."

The figure said no more.

Daniel spoke first. "We'd like to read the story of Vindictus Sharpe please."

Behind the white hood, the figure gave a nod. It stepped onto the boat, and motioned for them to follow. As the boat moved off, Daniel dipped a hand into the black liquid, rubbed it between his fingers. It really was ink.

The boat moved between great mountains of books, beneath archways and tunnels carved through the bookcases.

"It's strange, isn't it?" said Ellie, her curls blowing in the breeze as the boat coasted on. "The story of everyone. Do you realise, Daniel, you could find your own book and read how you're going to die?"

Daniel swallowed.

"I think I'll leave it as a surprise."

The boat docked in one of the narrow canals, between two bookcases hundreds of metres tall. High above, several rope bridges crisscrossed.

The hooded librarian led the way from the boat, hopping onto the wooden platform at the foot of the bookcase and up the first staircase. The climb was steep. Daniel's legs were burning when the librarian called a halt at last.

"Where is he?" asked Ellie anxiously. "Where's Sharpe's story?"

The librarian strode to the bookcase, reached out, and pulled a very fat volume from the shelves. The cover was black leather, and the pages leafed with gold. On the cover, serious-looking golden letters spelled out Vindictus Sharpe's name. The librarian reached out a hand, and offered the book to Daniel. It was heavier than he thought it would be.

He began to flip through the pages, but as he tried to read, it became obvious that something was very wrong. Words were moving on the page, disappearing and shifting and merging with other words. The whole book was a jumbled, wild tangle of letters.

"It doesn't make any sense," he said, handing the book back. "What's wrong with it?"

The librarian looked through the book. A pause.

"This person … has committed atrocities," it said. "He has taken from others. Stolen time. He has torn and warped his own life … his soul … so much that it has become unreadable."

"Brilliant," said Daniel. "We're stuffed."

"Maybe not," said Ellie.

"How do you mean?"

Ellie was half smiling. "Well, this library has the story of everyone, right?"

"Correct," said the librarian.

"So … that means Papa is in here too."

Daniel shook his head.

"Ellie, I think I know what you're thinking. It's not a good idea."

"Why not? If Papa's story is here, we can use it!"

"But if we search for him, we could lead Sharpe straight to him," said Daniel. "He's hiding for a reason and we need to trust him. I almost got swallowed by a door full of bony hands last time I tried something like that."

"I'm not talking about finding him," said Ellie. "I'm talking about reading his life to see what it says about Sharpe."

Daniel smiled.

"I know," said Ellie, "I'm a genius."

"Wouldn't go that far," said Daniel. Then he turned to the librarian and said, "Could you take us to the story of Lucien Silver please?"

Mr Silver's story was not as long as Sharpe's, which only proved to Daniel just how long Sharpe's past stretched back. When the librarian pulled it from a shelf in the remotest of bookcases and handed it to Ellie, she wasted no time in leafing through the pages.

"How far do you think I should go? Papa's quite old…"

A great rumble filled the air. Several books fell from nearby bookcases.

"Um. Ellie. Flip faster."

"Yeah, yeah, give me a sec."

Another rumble, and the sound of distant splashing. The ink was growing choppy.

"What's happening?" asked Daniel.

The librarian raised a hand. "I do not know."

And then the hand was gone, and the librarian's robe was filled only with black ink, soaking into the white material. The empty robe crumpled, the ink splashing back on Daniel and Ellie, who looked at each other with wide eyes.

"The library's falling apart!" said Daniel. "We need to get out. Now."

When they climbed back into the boat, the wind gathered pace, blowing stronger and stronger, whistling through the bookcase canyons, whipping the surface of the ink canal. The boat was tossed around like a toy. There were great groans and splashes from deep in the library. The boat bobbed in the swell as Daniel grabbed the oars and began to row. Then, as they hit the open water in the centre of the library, there was another rumble. Behind, a great mountain of books was collapsing, like a glacier, into the ink. As the weight crashed into the surface, a tall black wave formed, tearing towards the boat.

The boat was lifted high, carried faster and faster. Daniel held on to the side and linked arms with Ellie. And then the boat was upturned, and everything was spinning, and there was nothing but cold, wet blackness.

Daniel's head broke the surface just as another wave crashed down on him, and he was pushed deeper into the ink. He felt like his lungs were about to burst. He did not know which way was up. The ink was thicker than water, and the weight of it seemed to be pushing and squeezing him. A desperate flailing of arms and legs, and he was back on the surface, gasping and gulping the cold air.

"Ellie!"

"Daniel! Here! Over here!"

He followed the voice, and spotted Ellie climbing up onto the wooden island that led back to the Emporium. Swimming against the tide was not easy. He knew at any minute he might be crushed like a bug by a falling bookcase. He tried to ignore the groans and creaks, and at last he reached out an exhausted hand and grasped Ellie's arm. He half climbed, was half pulled from the ink.

To the doorway they fled, ducking as wild books tore through the air overhead. Then the door was open, and they were falling onto the cold Emporium floor, scrambling up to push and push with everything they had against the door. As they fought the wind, a mountainous bookcase pounded into the water, a gigantic wave rose from the surface and swept towards the door. Daniel's eyes widened, and he pushed harder. The door began to give, inching closed as the wave hurtled towards them…

The door slammed shut. The crashing wave roared against the closed doorway, making the entire Emporium shake. Far away, in the hall of staircases, several sets of stairs collapsed to rubble.

Daniel and Ellie fell to their knees, panting, covered from head to foot in ink.

"I lost Papa's life story," said Ellie.

"At least we're alive," said Daniel. He reached into his coat pocket and pulled out the *Book of Wonders*. Though he was soaked through, and his skin and clothes were stained with black ink, the book looked somehow untouched.

"I guess it's back to the drawing board. I just wish someone would help us, someone who really knows every part of the Emporium."

He opened the *Book of Wonders* at a random page and skimmed the contents. After a few pages of nothing particularly helpful, a familiar chattering interrupted the silence. A flash of silver. The surviving magpie hurtled towards Daniel. He ducked his head as it swooped, knocking the book from his hands.

"Hoi!"

The bird paid him no attention. It landed on the

open pages of the book and sat as if it were incubating a clutch of eggs.

"Away you go," said Daniel. With a half-hearted wave, he dislodged the bird. It hopped to the side of the book and twitched its head towards the open page, then fixed Daniel with a ruby stare. He gazed past the bird, to the page, and narrowed his eyes. Then he picked up the book and read. After a moment, he smiled a small smile. He stroked the magpie's head.

"Clever girl," he said. "Thank you."

Then he turned to Ellie, who had been watching with bemusement, and said, "I know where we have to go next."

CHAPTER 31

MEMORIUM

On route to their destination, Daniel and Ellie made one detour, visiting Mr Silver's apartments and collecting a long brown hair from his pillow. The hair was not difficult to find. Mr Silver had enough of them, after all.

"The *Book of Wonders* says we need one of his hairs for this to work," said Daniel. "I'm not really sure why…" he squinted at the page in question. "His writing gets pretty bad sometimes. I guess there's only one way to find out."

The Emporium was becoming impossible to navigate safely. Patches of creeping nothingness were appearing more and more, sucking Wonders into the void, weakening the rest of the Emporium, which was decaying like a row of bad teeth. Not only were there dangers in the form of fallen bridges, caved-in passageways and flooding tunnels, but Daniel also found that his sense of direction was almost completely gone. Thankfully, the surviving Magpie became a guide.

When they arrived at the door, in a corridor full of mirrors, Daniel leaned close to the gold nameplate.

"Memorium. This is it."

From somewhere deep in the Emporium came a rumble. The floor trembled. Daniel ran his fingers along the wall, tracing hairline cracks.

Through the door lay a movie theatre with a carpet the colour of fresh blood, and row upon row of seats padded with red velvet, all facing a huge screen.

Something happened to the air beside Daniel, and the shadows moved, turning into the shape of a man. The man was tall and gaunt, with sandpaper-rough skin and a patch over his left eye. He wore a black uniform with gold piping and carried a torch. He smelled of dust and sugar.

He said, "I am your usher for this evening. How may I be of assistance?"

"Erm … how does this work?" asked Daniel.

The usher smiled.

"We show you the past, plucked from memories. The true past, mind you, not coloured by bias or age or worn away by time. Everything, exactly as it happened. The price is a single hair."

"What we want to see…" said Ellie, "it's not our own past. It belongs to someone else."

The usher's good eye flicked between Daniel and Ellie.

"Do you have a hair that belongs to this person?"

They nodded.

"Then we do not have a problem," said the usher. "Take a seat if you please." He led them to the front row, directly beneath the screen, and signalled that they should sit. He held out a hand. "Payment."

Ellie took Mr Silver's hair from her pocket, placed it in the usher's hand. He brought it up close to his good eye. Then he took off his hat, revealing the strangest head of hair Daniel had ever seen. A large section of his head was completely bald. But there were places, here and there, where hair sprouted. The hair was many different colours and many different lengths.

The usher took Silver's hair. He produced a sewing needle from the pocket of his uniform. He threaded the hair through the eye of the needle. Then he raised the needle to his head, pressed the end into his scalp, and proceeded to sew Mr Silver's hair into his own head. When he was satisfied that the hair was in place, he replaced his hat and sat in the empty seat next to Daniel, who had watched all of this with horrified fascination.

"Now we can begin," the usher said. "What exactly would you like to see?"

"We need to find out the story between Mr Silver and Vindictus Sharpe," said Daniel. "Anything from Silver's memories that can help us understand Sharpe a little better – and if there's anything in there we can use against him, all the better."

The usher gave a thoughtful nod.

"Very well."

He sat back in the chair beside Daniel, raised a hand to his face, and lifted his eye patch.

Daniel could not help looking; he caught a glimpse of the usher's hollow eye socket, just as the lights of the theatre died away, leaving the place in darkness. Then the usher's body straightened out, became rigid, and a beam of white light erupted from his empty eye socket and thundered onto the screen.

A crackling noise tickled Daniel's ears, like the scratching of a record. The screen was filled with flashes of white, which slowly resolved into a grainy picture: a snow-covered city in the dead of night; a lone figure climbing the steps of a serious-looking building covered in gargoyles…

…and they saw it all: Lucien Silver, the frightened little boy teased by the other children, rescued from loneliness and torment by a mysterious stranger on a freezing Edinburgh night. The years of teaching, of perfecting the art of magic, of mistakes and missteps punished by beatings, and rainy days spent gazing through the narrow windows of a mansion, wishing that he did not have the gift, longing to be like everyone else.

The scene shifted. Lucien gave his first performance in the grand sitting room of a townhouse, in front of only Sharpe and an old woman named Birdie.

And then the performances began. A whirlwind lifestyle of travel and fame. Packed theatres across the globe were transfixed by the magic of Sharpe and Silver. But it was easy to see that a shadow was growing in Sharpe's heart, fed by jealousy of his protégé's talent. Lucien's invention of the *Book of Wonders* seemed to be the final blow, and by the time Daniel and Ellie had watched Birdie's funeral, Sharpe had abandoned Lucien, cast him back to the harsh reality of the world.

A cloud of steam filled the theatre, and when it had cleared, the screen showed Edinburgh once more. Lucien Silver stepped from a train, and he was much more like the Mr Silver that Daniel knew, confident and proud. When he opened the doors of his Emporium for the first time, his customers were afforded a view of a magical world unlike anything they had ever seen.

And then Sharpe was back, and Silver was walking the Emporium arm in arm with Michelle, and he was happier than Daniel had ever seen…

But the good times did not last.

Daniel gasped when Michelle betrayed Mr Silver.

Ellie grabbed his arm tight when she witnessed her father drop to his knees, his *Book of Wonders* gone, stolen by the love of his life. Ellie's grip only tightened when Silver answered the door on a rainy night one year later to discover a baby on his doorstep, a note slipped between the blankets.

Next they were following Lucien as he strode with purpose up a street lined with maple trees and huge houses. Lucien paused at the gates of the largest house, beside a nameplate bearing the name Vindictus Sharpe. He stared through the bars. Then he ran his fingers over the locks, and the gate was open, and Lucien was striding up the steps towards the front door…

Something happened to the picture then. It began to stretch and distort and break apart. There was a familiar face, a sneering Vindictus Sharpe who made them jump in their seats, and after that neither Daniel nor Ellie could make out anything besides the muffled sound of voices, and a scream, and a flash of red…

The lights of the theatre blinked softly back to life, casting the place in a warm amber glow.

"What happened?" said Daniel. "We need to know what happened next!"

In the seat beside him, the usher, whose expression

had been vacant throughout the showing, blinked his good eye. He sat up. He replaced his eye patch and gazed around the theatre as if seeing it for the first time. Then he looked at Daniel, and his eyebrows knitted.

"Well, that's never happened before," he said, removing his hat and scratching at the patchwork of hair on his scalp.

"Put it back on!" said Ellie. "Fix it!"

"Can't do it," said the usher. "There's no way to play back the final scene. It has been tampered with. Someone does not want it to be seen, simple as that. Whatever it is you wished to uncover, I'm afraid it's going to remain a secret."

Something stirred in Daniel's brain…

A secret.

The world faded around him. In his mind, he was no longer in the theatre. He was back in his early days at the Emporium, on the night he first wrote in the *Book of Wonders*.

Back in a room full of secrets.

"*May I have the honour of leaving the first secret in this room?*" Mr Silver had asked.

Daniel leapt out of his seat, grabbed Ellie by the arm, and began to pull her back up the aisle towards the exit.

"Daniel, let go! Would you please tell me what is going on?"

They clattered out of the door, leaving the old theatre in silence once again.

The usher climbed from his seat, and watched after them. He scratched his chin.

"What a strange pair," he said. The lights died once more, and with a flutter in the darkness, he was gone.

CHAPTER 32

SILVER'S SECRET

Daniel had not visited the room of Secrets since the night he first scribbled it into the book. He feared that it might have crumbled away, and he was relieved to find it still standing. Most of the snow globes were still empty, but there were a few, scattered here and there, that had been filled by customers. Their secrets lay inside the glass domes: a single white flower, a torn love heart, a clockwork bird, waiting like lost treasures.

"So every one of these is a secret?" said Ellie, plucking a globe from the column and stuffing it straight back when she realised that it contained a miniature skull.

Daniel began to climb the steps, winding up and

around the column, searching the secrets with his eyes.

"Yup," he said.

"So what are we looking for?"

"I don't know exactly. I'm hoping I'll know it when I see it." He had forgotten just how many snow globes there were; thousands of them twinkled in the dim light. His eyes scanned every one of the glass spheres as he wound up the steps, careful not to miss anything.

And then, there it was, nestled among hundreds of empty globes. When Daniel's eyes found it he knew that it was right. He reached up and gently lifted the secret from its place, then carried it back down the steps. He held it out in an open palm.

"We're looking for this," he said. "It belongs to Mr Silver." He held the globe up. "You saw the film in the Memorium. Silver doesn't want anyone to know what happened the night he went after Sharpe. I'll bet that's the secret he left in this globe."

Daniel raised the globe above his head, and brought his hand down as hard as he could, throwing the glass orb to the floor, where it bounced and rolled away. He went after it, and picked it up, examining every millimetre of the glass.

"Not even a scratch," he said. He tried throwing Mr Silver's secret against the walls. He stamped on the thin glass. He even tried smashing two secrets together. Nothing worked. The globe remained whole. Daniel yelled in frustration and tossed the secret away.

"Daniel, stop!" said Ellie, stepping in front of him before he could try to break anything else. "Just stop."

Daniel's shoulders slumped. He looked around the room.

"I'm sorry. I just thought there was a chance, with the Emporium losing its power, that the secrets might not be safe any more. That the snow globes would be weak." He sat down, still out of breath. "We need to find out what happened that night, Ellie. It's the key to everything. I feel it."

Ellie's grey eyes suddenly opened wide. "Of course!"

"Of course what?" said Daniel.

"We've totally missed something," said Ellie. "We've been thinking about Papa's secret all wrong, approaching it as if he's the only one who knows what happened. But he's not, is he? There were *two* people involved."

Daniel stared up at her, feeling a wide smile spreading across his face. She was right: whatever Mr Silver was hiding, Vindictus Sharpe knew about it too – and that meant they could use Sharpe's memories to unlock the mystery.

"You know what?" he said. "I was wrong earlier. You are a genius."

"I know," said Ellie. "One problem though: we need a hair from Sharpe's head to make this work."

Daniel had to admit, this was a sticking point. It wasn't as if Sharpe would pluck a hair from his own head and hand it over with a smile.

"We'll figure it out," he said, and they headed for the door. "By the way, I've been meaning to ask: in the Memorium, when we watched Mr Silver's past, it showed a baby being dropped off on the doorstep of the Emporium. Was that ... that wasn't..."

"Me?" said Ellie. "Of course it was."

Daniel paused, confused. "But ... all that seemed to happen a long time ago."

Ellie nodded. She smiled, although it was not a happy smile.

"You know the birthday ball Papa threw for me – the one celebrating my twelfth birthday?"

"Yeah?"

"Well, that was the 121st time I've turned twelve."

Daniel blinked.

"You've been here that long?"

"I have."

"And you've never ... there's never been ... you haven't got any older? Not even a single day?"

"Papa let me grow up just enough that I wouldn't be under his feet all the time. But he didn't want me to go out into the world on my own. Now we know why. As long as I was in the Emporium he could protect me from Sharpe. So he put the shop in its own little bubble, with its own rules, its own time, totally separate from the world outside. And that's why I've been the same age for so long. People don't age here."

"That means … me too?" said Daniel. "If I stay here I'll never get any older?"

"Time only passes normally when you go outside," said Ellie. "It'll take you ages to grow up."

"I can't believe Mr Silver didn't tell me!" said Daniel. "I mean, he mentioned that he hadn't aged for a long time but … He should have told me!"

Ellie frowned. "Would it have changed your mind? Would you have come to work here if you'd known?"

"If I'd known I'd turn into Peter Pan?" said Daniel. "The boy who never grew up? I don't know. Maybe."

A deep growl reverberated around the place, like the rumbling belly of a hungry giant. The floor trembled, and the snow globes rattled in their places. Several secrets fell from the column. Daniel wondered how many Wonders had just disappeared forever.

Together they scurried away, leaving the door to the room of Secrets to click quietly shut.

CHAPTER 33

SPLITTING HAIRS

The magpie landed on Daniel's shoulder, slapping him on the side of the face with the piece of black card in its beak. On the back of the card, there were three words, written in a hurried scrawl in gold ink:

He's asleep. Hurry!

Daniel stowed the card in his pocket and began the short walk from his wagon, through the hall of stairs, to the red curtain. The plan was simple, as plans go; in fact, it had barely been a plan at all. Ellie was a ghost to Sharpe. She could watch him, and he would be oblivious. But she could not touch him. She could not be the one to take the hair from his head. That job would have to belong to Daniel. And so Ellie would watch Sharpe, wait until he was asleep, and alert Daniel, who would then sneak in and cut a hair from his head.

When he arrived at the curtain, Ellie was waiting. She did not look happy; there was a strange look in her grey eyes and she was staring off into space.

"Are you OK?" Daniel said in a low whisper.

Ellie started. "Yes. I think so. He's sleeping, but he's been sitting at Papa's desk all night, drinking whisky and throwing knives at the stuffed polar bear. Be careful, Daniel. He's not right. If he wakes up, he'll slit your throat."

The shop front was warm and calm. The only sounds in Daniel's ears as he crept towards Silver's desk were the pounding of his heart, and the snap and pop of the fire.

Sharpe was slumped over the desk, head resting on one arm. The other arm was strewn across the table, hand clutching a large silver dagger. Beside him on the table sat a whisky bottle containing only a few amber drops. In the far corner of the room, the stuffed polar bear was stuck with three knives, two in the chest and one between the eyes.

Daniel was at the desk now, crouched so that his chin was level with the desktop, affording him a view of the top of Sharpe's head. He reached into his pocket with great care, and slowly, gently, brought out a pair of scissors. Then, holding his breath, he leaned over the desk, touching the scissors to Sharpe's short hair. Several silver hairs fell to the desk, glinting in the firelight.

Daniel placed the scissors back in his pocket and, with trembling fingers, reached out to collect the hair.

His arm brushed against the whisky bottle. He froze, watching in horror as the bottle spun on its base, and then toppled, landing on its side with a loud clink. Sharpe gave a huff and a snort, and opened one electric-blue eye.

Daniel was glued to the spot in terror. He stared into the blue eye, waiting for the other to open, and for Sharpe to spring from his chair and gut him like a fish…

But he did not. The blue eye rolled back in its socket, the eye closed, and Sharpe began to snore. Daniel stowed the hairs in his pocket, and crept away with as much stealth as he could.

Back on the other side of the curtain, Ellie gave him an expectant look, the magpie hopping on her shoulder.

"Well?"

Daniel smiled, held out his hand.

"Got it."

The magpie seemed to know what was going on; it twirled and looped through the Emporium, calling out in exited chatters as it led the way back to the Memorium.

Inside, the theatre lay silent and still. A patch of darkness fluttered, and the usher stood beside them once more.

"Ah, back again, are we? I told you, there's nothing I can do with the past I showed you. The event, whatever it was, shall remain a mystery."

"Someone else was there," said Daniel. "The past belongs to that person too." He held out his hand. "We've got another hair."

The usher snatched the hair, and held it to his good eye.

"Well, why didn't you say so?" he said, and he opened his arms, indicating the theatre. "Please take a seat."

They sat at the screen as the usher sewed Sharpe's hair into his head. Then he sat, and flipped up his eye patch. The beam of light erupted from his empty eye socket and found the screen.

An image crackled to life. Daniel and Ellie sat back, and they watched the truth at last.

CHAPTER 34

BAD BLOOD

Vindictus Sharpe opened his arms and soaked in the applause of the audience, who cheered and whistled and stamped their feet, blown away by the show.

When the curtain closed, Sharpe walked in silence to his dressing room. He poured himself a large whisky and gulped it down. Then another. He put on his coat and gloves and scarf, and left the theatre through the stage door. The autumn air was cool and crisp; his breath danced around him as he walked the short distance to the grand house that he called home whenever he happened to be in Edinburgh, which was not very often these days.

No one met him at the door upon his arrival. He preferred to keep no staff. He removed his coat, and walked up two flights of stairs to his office. A half-empty bottle of whisky sat at his desk, beside a crystal glass. He poured a drink and sat at his desk. Then he reached into his pocket and brought out a book with a battered leather cover, placing it with care on the desk. He lit a desk lamp, stretched his fingers, and began to read through the pages, his eyes taking in every detail.

"It will never work for you as it does for me."

Sharpe knew the voice. He did not look up from the *Book of Wonders*.

"Lucien. Would you like a drink?"

Lucien Silver stood at the entrance to the room, grey eyes fixed upon his book.

"You used Michelle – your own daughter – to get to me. To get the book."

This time, Sharpe's eyes left the pages.

"Yes," he said.

Silver stepped further into the room.

"Why? Why steal the book? You know it will never work properly for you unless I give it up, or you challenge me and defeat me for it. And I will never give it up. There's too much of my soul in those pages. The book is as much a part of me as my heart. I live inside it."

Sharpe let the question hang in the air. He bit his lip, and his big hands trembled with anger.

Silver smiled as realisation dawned.

"You stole the book because you wanted to copy it!

That's it, isn't it? You want one for yourself, but you can't understand how it works. The book is beyond your talents, and it's eating you up. Ha! The great Vindictus Sharpe, reduced to imitation!"

He stepped forward again, so that he was now directly opposite the desk. "So where is it? Where is your version of the *Book of Wonders?* Weren't you able to create one?"

Sharpe stared at him with dangerous blue eyes. His lip curled into a sneer. "I have no time for such games."

Silver held out a hand. "Give me the book and you will never hear from me again."

Sharpe snapped the book shut, and rested a hand on its cover.

"Get out."

Silver leaned over the desk, his face close to Sharpe's.

"I am not leaving without my book. I have no wish to harm you, despite the fact that nobody could blame me if I did."

Sharpe did not answer. The book trembled beneath his fingers. He lifted his hand, and it flew off the desk, into the waiting grasp of Silver.

"Thank you," said Silver. "You will not see me again. Goodbye. And good luck."

He had reached the door when Sharpe spoke.

"I challenge you."

Silver stopped. He hung his head.

"Do not do this, Vindictus."

"I challenge you," repeated Sharpe. "No funny business. No messing about. A duel to the finish – the way things should be settled – until either one of us submits, or is killed in the process. If I win, the book belongs to me."

A pause.

"And if you lose?" said Silver.

Sharpe shrugged his great shoulders.

"I will leave that up to you," he said. "It will not happen in any case."

Silver thought for a moment.

"Years ago, at Birdie's funeral, you never answered when I questioned you about why you never age. I was right, wasn't I? You steal years from other people. Take away chunks of time from their lives. You eat their tomorrows."

Sharpe nodded.

"There are branches of magic that require … sacrifice."

"And it is wrong," said Silver. "It is delayed murder. If I win, you will stop it."

Sharpe stood his full height, a great bear of a man.

"And what are their lives compared to mine? What have they accomplished? They are oblivious to the possibilities this world can offer. Surely it's not too much to ask that a few of them should meet their maker a year or two early in order that I might continue my work?"

"There are other ways," said Silver. "Different paths to take. Other energies you could mine. Imagination, for one, has limitless potential. But you can't see that because you are a maniac." He paused. "I accept your challenge."

No sooner had the words left his mouth than Sharpe was upon him, flashing across the room, throwing him against the wall. Sharpe lifted Silver with a single hand, pushed him back against the wall and punched him hard in the gut, folding Silver in two. Then, with a wave of his hand, Sharpe lifted his desk from the floor and sent it hurtling across the room. Lucien dodged out of the way, just as it crashed against the stone.

The sound of cracking glass made Lucien look to the window, where a pane of glass splintered into shards and flew towards him. He tried to bend them around his body, but there were too many, and several slivers stabbed him deep in the leg.

He limped out into the hallway, down a set of stairs. Sharpe stalked after him, a savage grin on his face. Lucien tried to buy a little time by bringing to life several figures from paintings hung around the hall. But as they attempted to block Sharpe's path, he swatted at them; they dissolved into globules of paint and fell to the carpet.

Then the duelling magicians were rolling down the stairs, a ball of flailing arms and snarling teeth. Sharpe tossed Silver clear across the hallway into a grand sitting room. Silver scrambled backwards, pointing to the fire. Tongues of flame jumped from the fireplace and wrapped around Sharpe, encasing him in a blazing shell. He roared, and the fire turned to smoke.

"You should not have come here tonight," he said. There were three daggers in his hands. He tossed the first at Silver, and Silver managed to bend it away towards a sideboard, where it became buried deep in the wood.

The second dagger hit Silver in the shoulder. He wrenched back his head and screamed in agony, falling to his knees.

"The difference between you and me," said Sharpe, "is that I am not afraid to end this fight." He raised the final dagger above his head. The knife left Sharpe's hand, and his aim was true. It spun through the air, handle over blade, as it had done so many times on stage.

Lucien stared at the spinning blade. Everything else faded away. From the edges of the world, he thought he heard a woman's voice, familiar, soft...

"Father? Lucien? No!"

With the last ounce of his strength, Lucien Silver deflected the blade. It veered away to the right, gleaming and shimmering.

Lucien had not seen Michelle Sharpe arrive at the door.

The knife struck her in the heart.

When she hit the ground, she was already dead.

The world seemed to stop.

Sharpe stood perfectly still, staring at his daughter's lifeless body. Lucien Silver's eyes widened. He howled in agony and despair. Ignoring the pain from his own knife wound, he dragged himself towards her, holding her head in his hands. She was wearing a white nightgown, now stained crimson.

"Give me the book, and I will not involve the police," said Sharpe.

Lucien stared up at him, grey eyes heavy with sorrow.

"We killed her!" he yelled. "She is dead, and all you can think about is a book?"

He ripped the dagger from Michelle's chest, leapt to his feet, and pinned Sharpe against the wall, fuelled by wild rage. He was dwarfed by Sharpe, but in that moment, with the shackles taken off, no control or fear to bind him, he was a giant.

Sharpe's blue eyes widened as the tip of the blade touched his throat. "*You* killed her, Lucien," he whispered. "I did not throw the knife in her direction. It's your doing."

Lucien shook his head. His breathing was harsh, desperate.

"No … no, I loved her! I would never hurt her!"

Sharpe stared at him, their faces only inches apart.

"Murderer," he whispered.

Lucien Silver dropped the knife. He stepped back, clutching at his hair and his chest.

"No. No!"

"Murderer," Sharpe said once more, and there was a terrible smile on his lips.

Lucien tore a clump of hair from his head. He felt the *Book of Wonders* in the pocket of his coat. He turned and glanced once more at Michelle's body.

And then he was gone.

"This is not finished!" screamed Sharpe into the night. "The duel is not finished! I will find you, wherever you go, and I will kill you and take the book!"

Calmly, coolly, he stepped over his daughter's body, opened a wooden cabinet, and poured himself a whisky from a crystal decanter. Then he left the room, leaving Michelle to stare sightlessly into the roaring fire.

CHAPTER 35

THE CHALLENGE

Daniel sat in stunned silence as the theatre lights came back up. He tried to wrap his head around what he'd seen, and once again, in the back room of his mind there was something jumping out at him, screaming to be noticed. An idea … a possibility…

Beside him, Ellie's shoulders were bobbing up and down, tears streaming down her cheeks.

"Ellie?"

"I can't believe it, Daniel. She died, all because of a book! You saw it. And Papa didn't mean to kill her…"

"Of course he didn't!" said Daniel. He shivered at the thought of Michelle lying dead on the floor. "Mr Silver didn't even want to fight! She was in the wrong place at the wrong time. Sharpe's the monster."

A sneer of disgust crept over Ellie's face. "He stepped right over her, like she was a piece of dirt. She was my mum! She was his little girl, and if he can do that to her, then what will he do to us?" Her wide eyes were miniature versions of Mr Silver's. "Daniel, that man's a monster. We've got to get rid of him and save Papa. Daniel … Daniel?"

Daniel's mind had been turning, cogs and gears clicking into place. The idea in his head had caught fire.

"Ellie," he said, "I realise I haven't been here very long, but I reckon I know how Mr Silver works better than anyone. Something he said in the film we just watched … it got me thinking. I can't be sure, but I might know where your papa is."

She stared at him. "You do? Where?"

"I can't tell you yet. It's safer if I'm the only one who's in on it. You're going to have to trust me. I have an idea. I'm going to ask you to do something. It'll be dangerous, but I think it's the only chance we have."

Ellie returned Daniel's stare, her jaw set.

"Anything," she said.

"Good," said Daniel. "First of all, I have to pay another wee visit to the room of Secrets."

Grey Manhattan rain pelted the sepia-stained window of the Nowhere Emporium. Vindictus Sharpe sat at

Mr Silver's desk, throwing three silver knives one after the other at the stuffed polar bear.

Back at the Fountain, when the boy had first snatched the book, Sharpe had given chase, determined to find him and squeeze the air from his lungs. But the infernal Emporium had sent him running in circles. He had returned to the shop front, deciding instead to wait the boy out.

A whisper from the red velvet curtain caught his attention, and he spun to see the boy standing straight-backed, defiant.

Daniel had never been as frightened of anything as he was of Sharpe. Nothing, not even Spud Harper and his gang, came close to the cold blue stare that was fixing him now. He made himself as tall as he could.

"I know where Mr Silver is hiding," he said.

Sharpe was upon him in a heartbeat, pinning him like a rag doll against the wall, a silver blade pressed to his throat. He took the *Book of Wonders* from Daniel's pocket and tossed it on the desk.

"Please elaborate," he said.

Daniel swallowed, tried to keep breathing.

"No. I won't."

The knife dug into his skin, but not quite enough to draw blood.

"I could torture you, you know," Sharpe said. "I could make you tell me."

Slowly, Daniel reached into his pocket. When he

pulled his hand out, a tiny snow globe sat in his palm.

Sharpe looked at it.

"Am I supposed to know what that is?"

"It's a secret," said Daniel. "It's the secret you want to know. It's where you can find Mr Silver. I figured it out."

Sharpe snatched the secret from his hand. Daniel relaxed a little as the knife was withdrawn from his throat. Sharpe shook the secret, held it to his ear.

"It won't work," Daniel went on. "That's the whole idea of a secret, isn't it? I don't want you to know where Silver is. And as long as the secret is in that globe, you can't force it out of me."

Electric-blue eyes flicked from the secret to Daniel. "Why did you come?"

Daniel shrugged. "To challenge you."

"Excuse me?"

"I know how it works. I know that if I challenge you, you either accept, or you give up. So I challenge you. I'll write a Wonder into the book just for you. Inside it will be your challenge. And you write one for me. We'll go in at the same time, and whoever comes out first is the winner."

Sharpe smiled. "If I win?" he asked.

Daniel pointed to the secret. "I'll help you find Mr Silver. I know you need him to die for the book to be yours. But he's not going to come out to play. You'll have to wait till the Emporium collapses on top of him, till it's totally dead – and that could take a long time. This way, if you win, you can kill him, and the book will be yours."

Sharpe nodded agreeably.

"And if I win," continued Daniel, "you leave us alone, and you don't ever come back." He held out a hand. "Agreed?"

Sharpe scratched the silver stubble on his chin. Then his hand swallowed the boy's, and an electric ripple passed through the room. "Agreed."

Daniel walked to the desk, trying to look more confident than he felt. As he picked up one of Silver's fountain pens, his mind began to fill with doubts. Would the Emporium support the creation of two new Wonders? Was his idea really as good as he first thought? What sort of challenge would Sharpe think up for him? What if he lost? He was gambling an awful lot on the belief that he was good enough to beat this man, that the Emporium would help him.

He opened the book to an empty page. "I'll link the doors, so they should appear together."

"Write away, Daniel Holmes," said Sharpe. "Write away."

Daniel gripped the pen tight so that his hand wouldn't shake. Then he pressed the nib to the page, and the ink began to flow.

CHAPTER 36

DANIEL VERSUS VINDICTUS

The doors did appear together, as Daniel had predicted.

Thankfully, the corridor in which the new doors stood was largely intact, though the first signs of familiar cracks were creeping into the polished slabs.

The doors were identical, arched and shining black, with a gold doorknob. The only difference between the two was the nameplates, each displaying the name of the challenger.

As Daniel placed the *Book of Wonders* on the floor between the two doors, he sensed suddenly that the corridor was filled with people. He straightened up, looked around, and his eyes widened.

The Emporium staff – at least those who were

able – had come. They stood side by side, shoulder to shoulder, a ragtag band of misfits, some dabbing black ink from their leaking noses, or leaning on their neighbours. Leading the pack, standing tall, was Caleb. He nodded to Daniel.

"Come on, Daniel!" he yelled, to a smattering of cheers.

"Show him who's boss!" said someone else at the back of the crowd.

"We believe in you!"

Daniel looked at Sharpe, and suddenly his opponent did not seem quite so huge, or his task so impossible. He nodded to the crowd, his friends, more thankful to have them with him than he could say. Then he said to Vindictus Sharpe, "Ready?"

Sharpe unfolded his arms and did not try to stifle the smug smile that crossed his lips. "Always."

They each turned to face the door that contained their challenge. They moved forward, and reached for the doorknobs. Then they opened the doors and stepped into the unknown.

Daniel was falling. The world around him was black and damp. He landed with a splash in a pool of water so cold that he thought his heart might freeze. Saltwater filled his mouth, spurted from his nose as he coughed and choked. Everything was swaying and lurching, up and down, up and down, turning his stomach. A flash of lightning lit up the world, cast light on a long narrow space with metal walls and bunks and a galley kitchen. He was in a boat. Realisation dawned on Daniel with a sickening lurch of his stomach. His feet barely touching the bottom of the pool, he struggled to a porthole, stared out at the black night.

Another fork of lightning. For half a heartbeat Daniel saw the sea, angry and swollen, waves like mountains crashing all around. He tried to be calm in the pitch black; the water was slowly rising, creeping like cold hands.

Feeling his way around, Daniel willed his eyes to see through the blackness. He tried to visualise a lamp, a torch, a floodlight – anything to help him see … He imagined himself striking a match, filling the boat with dancing yellow light, and as the picture filled his head, something dropped into his pocket. He reached down and pulled out a box of sodden matches. Desperately, he struck one of the matches and was amazed when it sparked to life, just as he'd imagined, casting a flickering glow around the tight belly of the boat.

He moved out of the galley, banging and stuttering as huge waves tossed the ship, to a narrow metal corridor, and found a black door with a golden handle. In his excitement he dropped his light, but when the match hit the cold surface, the flame did not go out. It remained lit. The match sank, as if it was made of lead, illuminating the black water as it drifted towards the floor.

He struck another match, the light dazzling his eyes in the dark of the corridor, and he reached for the door.

Sharpe has underestimated me! he thought as his hands closed around the handle.

But something groaned, loud and metallic and old. There was a ping, and the ship juddered and shook and swung. The sound of rushing water filled Daniel's ears, and he held on tight to whatever his grasping hands could find as the boat began to tip up, to fill with water.

The floor became steeper and steeper, climbed and climbed until it was vertical, and all the time the doorway back to the Emporium, to Ellie and Silver and his home, was being submerged, deeper and deeper. Water was spraying everywhere, catching Daniel in the face, filling his mouth and nose.

He fell, tumbling, catching his elbow on the metal walls, and landed with a splash in the rising water, water that would soon fill the entire corridor, the entire ship.

Sharpe's cruelty shone through, bright as one of Daniel's matches. The idea was simple, and brilliant. If Daniel were to escape, he'd have to face his biggest fear and avoid the same death that his father had suffered, alone in the dark with nobody's hand to hold.

Sharpe's door also led to darkness, though the absence of light did not last. Bright lights flickered on all around him, dazzling and familiar. Stage lights.

The lock on the exit clicked shut.

He stood on a grand stage, with curtains of black velvet and a floor of polished mahogany. The place seemed vast, though it was difficult to tell – dazzling lights shone at him from out in the theatre, making it impossible to see the audience. But there was an audience there; he could sense it, even if they were oddly silent and still.

"This is my challenge?" he asked, flashing perfect teeth. "To perform? To amaze?" He laughed, wondering exactly what it would take to unlock the door. Perhaps some sort of approval from the crowd? Since the boy would soon be dead, it hardly mattered, but something about being on stage again, performing, appealed to him.

He took off his coat, and threw it in the air, where it became black smoke and evaporated. He looked to the audience. Silence. Perhaps pleasing this crowd would be more challenging than he thought.

He tried again, firing a bullet from a gun and catching it across stage. The crowd was still.

Sharpe shook his head and cursed.

"What do you people want?" he yelled.

Something broke the silence, the voice of a young girl.

"Let him see me," the voice said. "For this to work, he has to see me. I'm asking for help, Papa. Please, let him know that I exist. No more ghosts. No more hiding. It's time to end this."

"Hello?" There was a hint of unease in Sharpe's voice.

Across the stage, towards the door, a girl appeared from nowhere. She had eyes the colour of thunderclouds – eyes he recognised – and a tangle of wild black curls.

"Who are you?" he asked.

She stood perfectly still, staring through him.

"My name is Ellie Silver," she said. "And I'm your granddaughter."

The boat was almost full of water. Daniel was freezing and weak from his efforts to swim down and budge the door. Each time he tried, the water was deeper, and so the swim to the bottom of the submerged passageway became more of a struggle.

This time, as he came back up, there was barely enough space to keep his head above the surface.

He did not cry, as he thought he might when he imagined the moment in his nightmares. He only thought of the Emporium, and Ellie and Mr Silver; how he'd let them all down if he failed. Another deep breath, another lung-bursting swim through the darkness, and again he could not move the door. He swam back to the surface, banging his head on the metal ceiling. His time was almost up.

If I do die here, he thought, *at least it will be fighting for something. At least I didn't sit back and do nothing.*

He thought of his mother and his father, and he wondered what happened when someone died, if he'd see his parents again, or if dying was like flicking a switch, and he'd be gone and forgotten and that was that.

His nose was pressed against the ceiling now. He was gasping for breath…

And then, as the water closed in around him, he had a thought, a memory … and he heard Mr Silver's voice as clearly as if he were floating beside him.

"If, by some curious twist of fate, you find yourself in trouble, the Emporium will help you. All you have to do is ask."

The water was in his mouth, in his ears and eyes.

"Help me," he said to the Emporium through a mouthful of freezing water. "Please, help me find my way back."

One last breath. Daniel felt the water envelop him. He dived, because he did not know what else to do. He swam to the door, began one last attempt to open it. His lungs burned. He fought and fought the overwhelming urge to breathe, ignored his body's desperate call for air. He began to fade...

And then someone took his hand in the darkness, and another hand was fumbling in his pockets, removing the matches. A flash of blinding light lit up the black, shaking Daniel back to life. Someone grabbed him around the neck, and he found that he was staring into a face that was both familiar and strange, framed by a mane of hair the same burning orange as his own.

The man took Daniel by the wrist and pulled him back towards the door. Then Daniel stared into his eyes, nodded, and began to pull on the door. Daniel's lungs screamed. The pain made his ears ring, and he saw flashes of light in the corners of his vision.

But the door was budging. Slowly, surely it was opening!

The man gave Daniel a smile, and nodded towards the door. Half in a dream, Daniel nodded back. He reached for the door with hands like lead, and he pulled...

The door opened. Daniel was sucked through the doorway, like a spider down the plughole. He landed hard, gasping cool fresh air into his lungs. Water was flowing down the corridor and away. The book of matches lay beside him, and he kissed them and stowed them in his pocket as the Emporium staff mobbed him. They picked him up and patted him on the back and called his name. Every breath was a welcome gift. He was back in the corridor. He was alive.

And he was quite sure that the ghost of his dead father had just saved his life.

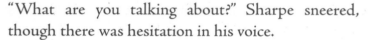

"What are you talking about?" Sharpe sneered, though there was hesitation in his voice.

Ellie took one step towards him.

"My papa told me that my mum left me on the doorstep of the Emporium in Edinburgh. He said she was a servant who wanted me to have a better life. I think the servant part was true. That's how you treated her, isn't it?"

Sharpe stayed very still.

"You are not real," he said. "This is a trick."

"Is it?" said Ellie. "I'm real; I promise you that. And I know all about you. You're a monster. You're dangerous. Papa has been protecting me from you all this time. He knew you'd take me away, treat me just like you treated her."

"Treated who, for pity's sake?"

Ellie pointed to the crowd. The lights that had been blinding Sharpe flickered out. He took a sharp breath, and a half-step back. There were a thousand seats in the theatre, and every one of them was taken by the same person: a young woman with red curls and porcelain skin, wearing a white nightgown dyed red with blood from the knife that was sticking in her heart.

"Michelle?" whispered Sharpe. His face was unreadable, but his voice shook.

"You treated her like dirt," said Ellie. "She was my mum, and you used her to break my papa's heart and steal his book. She hid away from you while you travelled and made your fortune, and she didn't tell you about me, because in the end she wasn't like you. There was good in her."

"What do you want me to say?" said Sharpe.

Ellie returned the cold stare. "Say you're sorry, and mean it. That's all you have to do to open the door. To win."

Silence. Sharpe stood centre stage, just the way he liked it. He smiled.

"I don't have to do a damn thing," he said. He motioned to the door. "Out there, through a door just like this one, Daniel Holmes is dying. When his body goes limp, and his last breath is gone, this door will unlock and the *Book of Wonders* will be mine."

No sooner had he finished speaking when the lock on the door clicked, and the door swung open. Sharpe's coat appeared in his hands, and he put it on and gave Ellie a cruel smile.

"You see?" he said. "It was only a matter of how long Mr Holmes could hold his breath."

"Actually, I'm quite good at holding my breath." Daniel was sodden. He stood at the door, the *Book of Wonders* in his hands. The smug look on Sharpe's face vanished.

"Impossible," he said.

Daniel raised a finger in correction. "You're in the Nowhere Emporium, Mr Sharpe. Nothing's impossible." He held up the book. "You lose. The book stays here, where it belongs."

Sharpe stared at Daniel, wild fury in his eyes.

"But ... there was no way out. How did you escape?"

Daniel patted the doorway.

"I know things you don't," he said, ignoring Sharpe when he scoffed. "I know that you and Mr Silver had a challenge of your own. I know that challenge never ended. Don't you see? We're a part of it, Ellie and me. Players in the same game. This was a challenge within a challenge. We were fighting for Mr Silver.

"So here's how it is: everything we agreed stands. You have to go, and never come back. But everything you agreed with Mr Silver all those years ago also stands. You have to stop stealing life from innocent people, stealing their time, their tomorrows. You have to grow old. And one day you have to die."

Sharpe spat on the stage floor. His face flushed brilliant red. "Where is he hiding?"

Daniel smiled. He held up the *Book of Wonders*. "In the book. He told you once that the book was part of him, part of his soul. You had the book in your hands, Sharpe. You had Silver in your hands, and you never knew. If you hadn't been so arrogant—"

Sharpe moved so quickly, a blur in the shadows.

Ellie screamed. Sharpe was behind her, holding her tight, a knife to her throat.

Behind Daniel, the crowd gasped.

"You have taken something from me today, Daniel Holmes. And *nobody* takes *anything* from *me*. So I intend to take something from you. The girl is my blood. She will come with me. Step aside or I slit her throat."

Daniel shook his head. "You don't understand, do you? The Emporium wants you to leave. I'd listen to it, if I were you."

Out in the theatre audience, the many versions of Michelle Sharpe left their seats and began to lumber towards the stage. They climbed the steps, the slow walk of the dead, and formed a ring around Sharpe.

"Stop this!" he yelled. "Stop it. I'll kill her!"

Cold hands wrapped around his wrist, prized the dagger from his grip. Ellie aimed a kick at his shins, squirmed free and wriggled through the crowd to Daniel.

"You took your time," she said. "Can we finish this now?"

Then they turned back to Sharpe, who was fighting through the crowd towards the door.

"I may have lost," he yelled, batting away one of the many Michelles, "but nowhere in our agreement did it state that I had to leave you in one piece."

He reached into his coat, and his blades gleamed in the stage lights. The first two daggers missed their target, plunging deep into the wall beside the door, level with Daniel's head. But Sharpe's third throw was true, and the knife spun through the dark theatre towards Daniel's heart.

A flash of silver, a chattering call, and the magpie swooped down in front of him, wings spread wide. The dagger hit the bird in the chest, and the magpie exploded in a cloud of rubies, raining to the ground with a sound like falling stars.

Sharpe let out a roar of anger. He ran towards Daniel, knocking many versions of his dead daughter out of his path, his teeth clenched, veins popping in his forehead and neck.

Daniel opened the book. He tried to stay calm as he found the correct page, and ripped it out. At once, the floor of the theatre began to break, to crumble and fall to infinite darkness.

The fury in Sharpe's face had been replaced by cold fear. He quickened his pace, leaping as sections of the floor disappeared beneath him. The Emporium's glittering bricks closed in around the door, suffocating the doorway. One final roar, and he leapt for the exit. But he fell short, and tumbled into the abyss as the door disappeared, sealing him in a nightmare forever.

The Emporium was silent. And then the staff roared, and Daniel and Ellie were surrounded by cheering people wanting to hug them, to lift them and carry them on their shoulders.

"Give them space!" cried Caleb. "They haven't finished yet!"

Daniel scrunched the page up. He handed it to Ellie, took the matches from his pocket, and lit one of them. Ellie held the page to the orange flame. They watched it burn together, until all that remained was a small pile of ash.

CHAPTER 37

PAGES IN THE WIND

The front of shop was still and silent. Everything about the place, from the teetering columns of books to the wondrous array of shimmering treasures and the warmth of the fire, remained unchanged from the very first time Daniel had stumbled through the doors.

He placed the *Book of Wonders* on Silver's desk, beside Sharpe's empty whisky bottle.

The air in the Emporium seemed to become heavy, like the air before a storm. The *Book of Wonders* trembled. The cover cracked open, slamming on the wooden desk. Pages flipped and fanned. A whistle sounded – the high-pitched shriek of a boiling kettle – and the book leapt high into the air.

Slap! It landed on the desk and lay still, open at the scorched pages.

Words began to form on the burned paper, tiny, black ink letters scrawling across the page. And then the words broke free of the page and floated upwards. They banded together, loops and flourishes of ink forming feathered tendrils that shifted and twined in the air like smoke. Details formed. The flash of a hand. What might be an eye. Slowly, surely, the words took the shape of a man. A man wearing a dusty grey suit. A man with thundercloud eyes, and a head full of wild, tangled brown hair: a living, breathing, solid person.

Mr Silver blinked. He rubbed a hand across his forehead and shook the cobwebs from his brain. He looked much older than Daniel remembered.

"Well," he said, "that stung more than I imagined."

Ellie leapt on him, knocking a cloud of dust from his suit.

"Papa! Oh Papa, Papa!"

Silver held her tightly. He placed his hands upon his daughter's face, wiped away her tears with his thumbs, and looked into her eyes, a mirror of his own.

"I am so very sorry that I left you. I promise there was no other way." He glanced at Daniel and said, "But you know that, don't you? You know everything."

Daniel said, "Sharpe told me that after such a long

time, the Emporium was becoming too much for you."

Mr Silver smiled, and his eyes were sad. "It began five or six years ago. At first, I barely noticed. But as time dragged on, I began to feel the strain, to feel my grip on the Emporium loosening. I knew that my powers were fading. And each time we moved on, I felt Vindictus Sharpe edge closer. There were a few very close calls. He almost caught up with us in Barcelona."

"And that's why you needed the unicorn blood, isn't it?" said Daniel.

"Initially, I intended to use it to prolong my life just enough to find a suitable replacement. But things moved too quickly. I was forced to act."

Daniel said, "I invited Sharpe into the Emporium, Mr Silver. None of this would have happened if I hadn't. I'm sorry."

Silver held up a hand.

"You, my boy, have nothing to be sorry about. Sharpe would have found a way in eventually. He had been watching us; he tricked his way into Ellie's birthday ball. And that's when I made the decision to go into hiding. Sharpe had remained strong by stealing other people's futures. In my weakened state I would have been no match for him; he would have taken the book, and the Emporium would have been lost. I used the unicorn blood and almost every drop of my remaining magical strength to place myself in the book. But I did not abandon you, despite how it might have seemed. I retained a link to the outside world – something small, something that wouldn't take too much effort to sustain. The magpies."

"You were the magpies?" Daniel said.

"Always," said Silver. "They were my eyes and ears. I realised as things unfolded that I would have to lead you to the truth about Sharpe – a terrible truth, a truth I would rather remained buried." Mr Silver looked at the floor then, and he seemed to Daniel to become a small boy, waiting to be scolded.

Ellie said, "It's true we saw everything. We saw what happened on the night you went to get the book back from Sharpe. But it wasn't your fault. You didn't kill her."

Silver looked up, and there were tears in his grey eyes. "For over one hundred years, I have been running from the past," he said. "It's a relief that you finally know the truth. I wish I could go back, Ellie, and change what happened."

"You can!" said Ellie. "You can do anything! Go back and stop Sharpe before he throws the knife! Kill him before he kills you!"

Silver looked almost tortured then.

"I'm not a monster, Ellie. And you know that's not how it works. If I change the past I change the present. We'll all be different people, shaped by different experiences. We won't exist as we do now. And I do not wish to lose the you that I know."

Ellie dabbed at her eyes with a knuckle. "Michelle was really my mum? And she just left me on the doorstep like a bag of rubbish?"

"Your mother was not a bad woman," said Silver with a shake of the head. "She was manipulated by a master. But she knew when you were born that she had to give you up. She didn't wish you to be treated as she had been, or worse, for you to be taken away from her and raised by Sharpe. So she brought you here.

"It was quite a surprise to find you on the doorstep. And Sharpe has always been the reason that I have insisted you cannot leave. It's not because I'm lonely. It's not because I don't love you. I love you most of all, Ellie, more than you can imagine. You are the one thing in this world that I have got right. As long as you remained inside the Emporium, I could ensure that Sharpe couldn't harm you, couldn't even see you. You have always been safe."

"Not if the Emporium falls apart around me," said Ellie.

Silver scratched his head.

"I would never have put you in danger like that! It was all in my note…" He stopped. "Ah. Yes. The note. Didn't quite work out as I'd hoped."

Ellie reached into her pocket.

"Oh. You mean this note?" She waved the scrap of paper. "The note that tells us absolutely nothing?"

Silver stared at it.

"Yee-ees," he said, plucking the note from Ellie's hand and sniffing the burned edges. "Got scorched along with the book. Bit of a mistake ... My plan was quite similar to Daniel's, as it turns out, and part of the note said that you are now free to leave the Emporium any time you wish." He smiled, and nodded towards the door. "There's nothing to hide from now. The world is yours."

Ellie's eyes bugged open. She looked at the door.

A familiar rumble came from behind the curtain. The shop shivered, and the flames in the fire dulled and hiccupped. Mr Silver staggered backwards, and then regained his footing and charged to his desk, picking up the book.

"We don't have much time. If the Emporium is to be saved, then it must be passed to someone else. Someone who is up to the challenge." He patted the battered cover. "When I first began my search for a successor, I never imagined that the book would choose someone so young." His hand rested on Daniel's shoulder. "What do you say, Daniel Holmes?"

The question was too huge to fit entirely into Daniel's head. It took him a long time to answer.

"Me? Take over the Emporium? I'm just a boy! I don't know how!"

"You were old enough and wise enough to defeat an ancient and dangerous man. And you will not be alone."

Another rumble. Silver folded into his seat, clutching at his chest.

"If I say no," said Daniel, "the Emporium will die. It's not a fair thing to ask someone."

Mr Silver said, "Everything has its season, Daniel. If today is the day that the Emporium passes into history, then it will certainly not be your fault. The blame for all of this lies with me."

Daniel's mind was bursting with questions, with ideas and fears and excitement.

"I ... I don't think I could do what you've done ... live like you've lived," he said. "I don't want to steal anybody's imagination."

Mr Silver held up his hands. "You won't need to. If anyone has the imagination to power the Emporium, it is you. My dear boy, I would never demand that you live with the mistakes I have made – and I have made many. It will be a clean slate. A blank page. Your Emporium. Your rules. Your life."

"I could be normal?" said Daniel. "I could grow up, and grow old, and pass the Emporium on to someone else when I think it's time?"

Silver smiled.

"Aye. I think that would be a very wise way to live."

Daniel's gaze found Ellie. He wondered what was going on in her head, how she felt about her father passing the torch to someone other than herself. And then, as though reading his thoughts, she gave him a smile, showing the gap between her front teeth, and a nod.

Mr Silver offered a hand.

"Do we have a bargain?"

"Will the staff be OK? Caleb and Anja and the others?"

"The ones who survived will stay with you," said Silver. He rubbed at his eyes. "But I'm afraid to say there is no bringing back those who perished. They came from my mind, my imagination. You will have to write some new staff."

Daniel thought about the vastness of the Emporium. The shop was many things. It was a magical place. A place where anything was possible. A place with the power to bring happiness to the hearts of those who visited, those who believed. But to Daniel, most of all, it was home. The Emporium was where he belonged, at last.

He shook Silver's hand.

As their fingers touched, Daniel felt a shiver run up his spine. Something seemed to wrap around him, like an invisible blanket, and then it was gone, and their hands came apart. The air between them crackled. Mr Silver handed Daniel the *Book of Wonders*, and as Daniel held it, the cracked and worn cover began to repair, until the leather was smooth and shining. The golden letters shone clear once more, only this time, the name on the cover was not Mr Silver's. Daniel stared at the inscription:

The Wonders of Daniel Holmes

"It's done," said Mr Silver.

Daniel felt it. He felt it in the same way you feel that someone is watching you, or that a storm is coming. He felt the Emporium in his chest and his head and his blood. It was a part of him, and he was a part of it.

Silver beamed at him, though there was sadness in his eyes. He held out a hand to Ellie.

"Would you like to take a walk together?" Silver asked, pointing to the exit.

Ellie stared at the door, and then at her father. She nodded. Silver took her hand.

"Are you coming back?" Daniel asked.

Silver did not have to utter a word to answer the question; his eyes told Daniel everything.

"We ... we're not coming back?" said Ellie.

Silver kissed his daughter's hand. "You may return, if you wish," he said. "You have a life to live, a canvas to paint. What you do is up to you. Grow old, Ellie. Fall in love and out of love and travel the world. You stand at the beginning of your path. But this will be my last walk."

Ellie pulled away from him. "What are you saying?"

"I'm tired, Ellie. More exhausted than you can imagine. The very last of my energy is about to run dry. When I walk out of the Emporium, away from the magic, I will not be able to hold myself together any longer. Nothing can stop it now."

"You can't go away!" said Ellie, her voice trembling, "I've only just begun to get to know you properly."

Mr Silver placed a gentle hand on her shoulder. "Ellie, I would very much like to take one walk in the fresh air with my daughter before my time is up. Please."

Ellie said, "Will it hurt? When you go?"

"I don't believe so. I like to imagine that it will be as pleasant as stepping from cold shadow into warm sunshine." He smiled, and winked an eye the colour of thunder. "Are you ready?"

"No. But I'll walk with you."

"And Daniel," said Mr Silver, "you will find help in the *Book of Wonders*. I have left an echo of my knowledge within the pages. It will guide you when you need it."

Daniel gave a nod. "Thanks," he said, and he meant it more than he had ever meant anything. "Thank you for everything."

Silver took his hat from the stand by the door,

placed it on his head, and tipped the brim towards Daniel.

"Thank you, Daniel Holmes. I wish you the adventure of a lifetime."

The bell sang as Silver opened the door to the perfect autumn day, a golden sun high in the powder-blue sky. Daniel watched as they walked through the door, and found himself smiling as Ellie took her first steps in the outside world.

They walked, father and daughter, hand in hand, up the street to the corner of the block, where the sunlight shone brightest upon the sidewalk.

Time seemed to slow in the bustling Manhattan street as Silver kissed Ellie on the forehead. He said something, and she nodded, and they hugged.

Then a breeze whispered between the buildings, and in the time it took to blink, Mr Silver was gone, leaving hundreds of blank book pages in his place, twirling and soaring around Ellie in the wind, flashing in the light of the autumn sun.

She watched the pages for the longest time, dabbing at her eyes, until the last of them had become nothing more than a speck in the sky. Then she turned and walked slowly back to the Emporium, where Daniel held open the door. She collapsed into her father's chair.

"Are you all right?" Daniel wished he had something better to say. A lot had changed, but crying girls still left him stumped.

She peeked at him from behind her hands.

"No. I'm not."

A pause.

"I saw my dad," said Daniel. "During the duel with Sharpe. He helped me. I know it wasn't him ... not the real him anyway ... the shop created an echo from my memories. I always thought I didn't remember anything about him. Turns out he's been with me all along. He always will be. I don't think I'll have nightmares any more."

Ellie gave him a smile. She wiped her eyes, and stood up. She made her way around the shop to the device that steered the Emporium, the one with the many rings and numbers.

"Where should we go then?"

Daniel narrowed his eyes. "We?"

"You heard Papa. He told you to go and have an adventure. So let's go! There's a big world out there, and it's ours – all of it."

"You'll stay?"

"I felt the sun on my face today, Daniel. The real sun! And I can feel it any time I want. Knowing I can leave – just knowing – that's enough for now."

Daniel couldn't contain his joy. Ellie could be impossible. She was maddening, and infuriating. But she was also loyal and brave. She was his friend – his sister – and he could not imagine a better one. He ran over and hugged her tight.

"Are you feeling all right?" she said.

Daniel thought about the question. He was nervous and terrified, excited and proud. He felt the weight of the Emporium on his shoulders, the pull of the world at his feet. He felt ready.

Most of all, he felt alive. He felt at home.

A smile danced on the edges of his mouth as he reached for a dusty old atlas and opened the pages.

And then Daniel Holmes and Ellie Silver began to argue, as only the dearest friends can, about far-off shores and exotic-sounding places, and where they might find their next great adventure.

Perhaps one day they will visit the place where you live.

Perhaps you will hear people whispering about the appearance of a strange shop built from bricks the colour of midnight. Perhaps you will witness the shimmering golden gate turn to dust, and the firework sign in the sky. And maybe, if you truly believe, you will walk through the red curtain, and witness the Wonders and secrets of the Nowhere Emporium with your own eyes.

But then again...

Maybe you already have.

THE WONDERS OF ROSS MACKENZIE

Meet Ross MacKenzie, award-winning creator
of the magical Nowhere Emporium...

Where did your inspiration for *The Nowhere Emporium* come from?

It's a bit mysterious, actually! The Emporium sort of popped into my head fully formed. I could see this strange old shop so clearly in my head, the sparkling black brick and the faded sign. I knew the shop never stayed in one place for very long, and of course I had to find out why, so I wrote the story.

What is your favourite room in the Nowhere Emporium?

Actually, my favourite place in the entire Emporium is the shop-front where Daniel first meets Mr Silver. It's dim and dusty and mysterious, filled with so many treasures and curiosities. I could spend days looking around!

What would you write in the Book of Wonders?

I'd have a library with every story ever written waiting on the shelves for me. But it would be a library with a twist: I'd be able to meet the characters from my favourite books face to face!

Actually, on second thought, this might turn out to be dangerous – the bad guys would probably try to escape and take over the world!

Ross is also the author of Zac and the Dream Pirates, *winner of a Scottish Children's Book Award.*

Read on to enter

Shadowsmith

Ross MacKenzie's
next brilliant book...

Chapter One

There were two men in the graveyard, under the stars.

Both were very tall and unnaturally thin, and wore black suits and long black coats. They walked through the oldest parts of the church grounds among overgrown weeds and tombstones so decayed that the names of those buried beneath had been lost forever.

"This way," said the first man, who was bald and had a large crooked nose. He led the way through a tangle of trees to a wild patch of ground covered by long grass. "Here."

The second man had a face full of sharp features and a head of straggly dark hair. "You're sure?" he said.

"Positive," said the bald-headed man. "Unconsecrated ground. There's witches here. I can smell 'em. Have you ever known my nose to be wrong?"

The dark-haired man looked around, and smiled. "I do like a good graveyard," he said. "Don't you just *love* a good graveyard, Brother Swan?"

Brother Swan, the bald man, rubbed his hands together. "I do indeed, Brother Swift. Reminds me of the old days."

"Quite so," said Brother Swift. "I mean, I remember a time when we had the power to turn countries and kings against one another just by whispering in their ears. How

I long for the days when we sent plagues crawling around the world just by blowing into the wind."

"All that lovely red blood," said Brother Swan. "All that delicious pain and suffering." He licked his lips. "But look at us now, brother – reduced to sneaking about in the shadows. Mother would be turning in her grave. If she had one."

"We won't be sneaking much longer," said Brother Swift. He shook his greasy head. "No. Soon we'll stand proud, and we'll unleash hell."

"Lovely," said Brother Swan. He stepped forward, reached into his long black coat and pulled out three black candles. He crouched down and twisted each candle into the ground. Next he struck a match and lit them, casting soft yellow light on the surrounding trees.

Then, together, the brothers began to speak.

If you had been there, in the darkness of the graveyard, you would not have understood what they were saying. The words they spoke were a strange collection of sounds, some soft and hissing, others sharp and cutting. All of the words were ancient.

As brothers Swan and Swift spoke, the air around them became heavy and crackled with static. The yellow flames flickered and danced and turned blue, then green, then red, bright as a flare. And then the red flames changed to black. If you could burn a shadow, this would be the colour of its flames.

They waited.

They did not move, did not speak.

The candles went out.

In front of Brother Swan and Brother Swift, a long, thin crack appeared. Not a crack in the earth, in the mud and the stone. No. A crack in the *world*. A crack in *everything*. And on the other side a faraway darkness so black it made the night in the graveyard grow darker. Thousands of creatures scuttled out of the crack in the world, tiny and inky-black, as if someone had lifted a stone and disturbed them.

And then the witches came.

Three shadows dragged themselves up and out of the fissure, standing in the moonlight in front of the two brothers.

Brother Swift twisted a lock of greasy hair around a long, skinny finger. "You'll do," he said. "You'll do nicely."

Brother Swan looked the shadows up and down. Their shapes shifted and warped in the dim light of the moon. "Be still, my dears," he said, "be easy. We've brought you back. Back to the world that didn't want you. The world that tormented and killed you."

One of the witches tried to speak, but her voice was nothing more than the sound of the night breeze in the long grass.

"Be calm," said Brother Swift. "Your strength will come back. And when it does it will be your turn. Your turn to get revenge, to make them suffer."

"We have a job for you," Brother Swan told the shadows. He smiled. "Now listen carefully, my dears, while I tell you all about the Shadowsmith..."

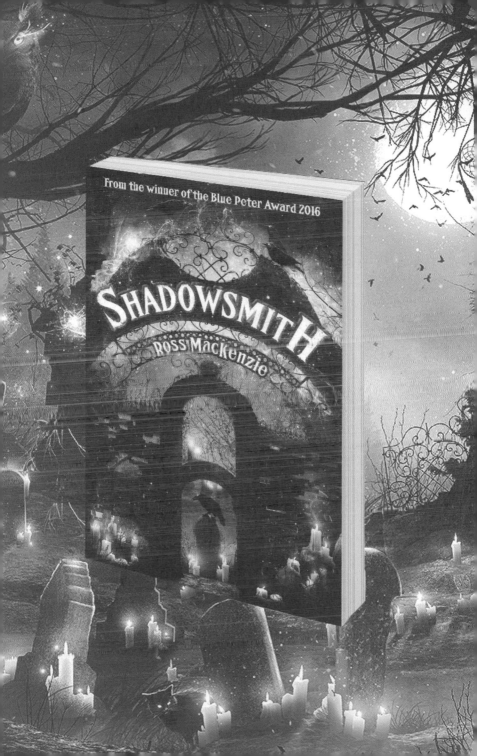